ALPHA'S BLOOD
A VAMPIRE SHIFTER ROMANCE

RENEE ROSE

LEE SAVINO

BURNING DESIRES

Copyright © April 2019 Alpha's Blood by Renee Rose and Lee Savino

All rights reserved. This copy is intended for the original purchaser of this book ONLY. No part of this book may be reproduced, scanned, or distributed in any printed or electronic form without prior written permission from the authors. Please do not participate in or encourage piracy of copyrighted materials in violation of the authors' rights. Purchase only authorized editions.

Published in the United States of America

Renee Rose Romance and Silverwood Press

Editor: Miranda Johnson

This book is a work of fiction. While reference might be made to actual historical events or existing locations, the names, characters, places and incidents are either the product of the authors' imaginations or are used fictitiously, and any resemblance to actual persons, living or dead, business establishments, events, or locales is entirely coincidental.

This book contains descriptions of many BDSM and sexual practices, but this is a work of fiction and, as such, should not be used in any way as a guide. The author and publisher will not be responsible for any loss, harm, injury, or death resulting from use of the information contained within. In other words, don't try this at home, folks!

❦ Created with Vellum

CHAPTER 1

Selene

THE STAGE IS an old battered platform, transformed by lush red curtains and glaring spotlights. How many Macbeths have died here? How many Hamlets? I wait in the wings, listening to the murmur of the audience. Goosebumps rise up and down my arms.

Relax, my mentor's voice whispered to me. *You're going to perform splendidly.*

I certainly hope so. I've trained for this moment my whole life. I'm wearing a strappy silky dress that drapes over my breasts and hips, molding to them with a nod to modesty while leaving my legs bare below mid thigh. The revealing attire doesn't bother me, but without weapons I'm naked. Since the age of sixteen, I've always had weapons on me. I used to fall asleep cradling my favorite: a wooden stake.

This is your greatest role. Your ultimate performance, my mentor said. *If you fail, you pay the ultimate price.* His voice deepened. *Do not fail me.*

I will not fail. After tonight, my life will hang in the balance, but that is nothing new. It always has. I've waited, and cried and sweated and fought and lived and breathed and died for this moment. The training demanded all of me, and I have given it my all. Whatever happens after tonight was plotted long ago, my part in the plot custom-made for me. I was born to play this role. Everything in my life has led to this moment.

"Ten minute warning," a black clad backstage hand calls. His gaze drifts over me like I'm a part of the set. I raise my chin and meet his gaze, staring until he drops it and scuttles away. I smooth my see-through garment and uncurl my lip. Tonight I pay a submissive part, but not until the curtains rise. I won't cringe before these cockroaches. I don't even bow to my mentor. It amuses him, my show of dominance. Or perhaps he thinks my alpha strength will protect me in my final mission. Either way, he allows my cheek. I'd be dead if he didn't.

Two shadows move in the depths of the stage. I don't bother glancing back. The guards are there for my protection, and to herd me onto the stage if I get cold feet. Unnecessary. I can't wait to play this role.

This old theater is long past its use. The air is dusty, stale. The green room holds another, sour scent that only grows worse when you descend the stairs into the basement filled with cages. My mentor hustled me past them, ordering me to focus on the endgame. A part of me wanted to turn and face the cages, find the ones that were full and break the bars. Free the frightened shifters. In another life, that would be my mission. Maybe it still can be—if I survive.

Will they end up on stage? I asked as we climbed the stairs, escaping those glittering eyes.

Some of them, my mentor answered. *Some of them are awaiting pickup.* He caught my anger and disgust and leaned close. *This is the perversion that Lucius Frangelico allows. When he is gone, we will right this wrong.*

It was the perfect thing to say. When I step on stage, all I will think about is the king sitting in the audience. The end of his reign will send shockwaves through his corrupt kingdom.

But first, Lucius Frangelico has to die.

He is here? Right now? I asked Xavier.

On his way, my mentor answered. *My spies report he will arrive in time. Once he is seated, we give the signal, and your part will begin,*

My fists clench at my sides and I force them to straighten. Time to get into my role. I must perform perfectly or I won't survive.

Another figure appears. An older woman emerges from the green room to give me a critical once over. I stand straight and let her study me. I even drop my eyes to the floor, acting like the submissive I'm supposed to be.

My hair is braided and pinned onto my head in a crown. I'm wearing minimal makeup: a hint of eye shadow, mascara, blush. Enough so the lights don't wash me out, with a bold touch around my mouth: the red, red lipstick. The color of blood and vampire dreams.

You will catch his attention immediately, my mentor

purred. *He will be pleased.* Xavier's eyes swept up and down my half naked form. I told myself his attention was impersonal, clinical, but couldn't help enjoying the approval glittering in his single eye.

And if he doesn't take the bait? I asked.

He will. If not tonight, one of my colleagues will purchase you and show you off. Wave you under Frangelico's nose. It is up to you to catch his attention. Xavier's large hands closed around my arms, his grip cruel and painful. His fingers left bruises, marks I accepted gratefully. My training didn't allow for comfort or friendly contact, but it left plenty of marks. I welcomed them like kisses or hugs. Pain became pleasure, and each bruise made me stronger, a honed weapon.

Xavier increased his grip, and I bit back a moan.

Good girl, he said, and my spirits soared. I wasn't sure if he meant to hurt me until he stepped back and let the makeup artist do her work. When she would cover the marks with makeup, he ordered her to leave them. *They catch the eye.* Xavier chucked me under the chin. *Remember all I've taught you.* I'd bowed my head and the one-eyed vampire walked off. The makeup artist shuddered, and I gave her a small smile of solidarity. Big, broad as a wrestler, with the ruined side of his face made barely presentable by an eye patch, Xavier was scary. He'd raised and trained me with unrelenting focus on my final goal: revenge. His methods were brutal and cruel. If he hadn't given me everything I'd need to avenge my slain pack, I'd hate him.

Maybe I do hate him. In my world, hate is an emotion not so far from love.

The makeup artist gives a brisk nod and walks off, her heels clopping on the scarred stage. With my eyes trained on the floor, I can't escape the signs of shifters—the shed fur, the scrapes on the floor where the guards forced the shifters onto the stage. The shifters who waited in the basement now, shivering in cages. I couldn't save them tonight. Maybe if I survive.

A flurry of activity in the wings, and a short bald man in a tux strides onstage, clutching a set of notecards. He flips through them, muttering under his breath. "Lot nine, special goods. She-wolf, trained, untouched. Unblooded." He glances at me, assessing. I might as well be a piece of meat.

I take a deep breath and get into character. Meek, submissive she-wolf trained to be a vampire's companion.

Frangelico won't be able to resist you, Xavier told me as he fastened a white collar around my neck. *You're beautiful.* It wasn't a compliment. In my world, beauty is a weapon. A weapon I was trained to use.

A stage hand hands the man in the tux a microphone.

"It's time," the auctioneer says and flaps his hand at me. I take a deep breath, raise my head, and glide barefoot onto the stage.

Lucius

"Sire, so good of you to join us." A bowing vampire

greets me as I step out of my limo. My bodyguards block his way until I motion them to step aside.

"I was told this is the place to buy a shifter." I survey the rundown building, the empty marquee.

"Yes, yes, you are correct." Dante gives a little laugh and runs to get the door. "The first half of the auction is over, but the remaining lots are sublime, I'm told. The *creme de la creme*. This way, please…"

I stride past the obsequious vampire. Why did I turn him? All my sired eventually disappoint. It's my curse.

Groups of well-dressed vampires discreetly watch me pass. I didn't expect to slip in unnoticed, but the way Dante keeps bobbing alongside me and babbling, I might as well have a spotlight shining on me.

The theater is old, but holds its own charm. A glass chandelier glows above my head. The red stage curtains have been brushed recently. But not even the strong cologne and perfume worn by the vampire audience can overpower the scent of shifter fur and fear.

I've been told the shifters are willing. Desperate for a protector, they agree to be sold to a vampire with a taste for shifter blood. There certainly are enough of us willing to pay good money for a pet.

"As you can see, our renovations have only begun. We've worked to preserve the integrity of the 1920s architecture—" Dante stops his tour abruptly when I lower myself into an aisle seat.

"Sire." His hands flutter in front of him. "We've prepared a seat for you in the middle of the aisle. This row has not been replaced—"

"It is fine," I nod to my protective detail and they take

up stations around the aisle I've chosen. Six of the best bodyguards money can buy, their weapons hidden under their suits. They're the guards people can see. I have more layers of protection than anyone can guess. After a thousand years of assassination attempts, one learns to plan ahead.

Dante hovers close, still trying to get me to move to a larger, newer seat. "These old seats have springs that aren't very comfortable."

He's right, one spring is digging into my backside at this very moment.

"I prefer this seat." I turn my attention to the empty stage.

Dust motes dance in the too-bright spotlights. The curtains ripple and the room fills with the audience's expectant murmur.

I stretch out my legs and ignore Dante's nervous hand fluttering. The fact that the vampire wants me to move hasn't escaped my notice. He keeps turning and signaling someone in the balcony.

My sired are plotting something. From the pains they took to stage this auction, their plot has been in the works for some time.

No matter. In my long lifetime, I've found one coup is much like another.

Theophilus, one of my sired, takes a seat a few rows ahead of me. He turns and bows his head. I tip my own in acknowledgement, and beckon him over.

"Sire," he says when he reaches my side, and bows. "How may I be of service?"

"How many auctions have been held here?"

He glances around the dimly lit room. "A fair amount. I only heard of them a few months ago. This is my third time."

"And the shifters are willing?"

"As willing as they can be." He grimaces. "Most are rare species. Without a large clan to protect them, they fall prey to stronger shifters."

"So they agree to this?" I wave a hand at the stage. "Is it better to belong to a vampire?"

"I am not a shifter, so I would not know. My guess is a life in servitude is better than no life at all."

I press my lips together. Most shifters I've met would rather be free. After all, they are part wild animal.

"Do you have any further questions about the auction?" Theophilus asks. Of all my sired, he's the least likely to conspire against me, but that doesn't mean he hasn't.

"Not at this time."

"Do you intend to bid, Sire?"

I study Theophilus' face for a hint of emotion. Interest, hope, anything. "I haven't decided." I give him an enigmatic smile.

"You might be surprised. Many of these shifters are naturally submissive. Owning such a powerful creature can be exhilarating."

"That is something to consider," I murmur.

"When you live forever, there are so few new pleasures to enjoy." Theophilus glances at the stage and licks his lips. A blatant show of anticipation.

Perhaps there is nothing nefarious about these auctions. In the long life of a vampire, it's easy to succumb to boredom. Boredom begets deeper and deeper perversions.

"When you live as long as I have, there are no new pleasures," I say. "You make do with the old."

Theophilus bows his head. "With all due respect, consider bidding tonight. Some of the shifters agree to the auction, but put up delicious resistance after they're bought. Subduing them provides months of entertainment, if you draw it out."

"Months? You surprise me, Theophilus," I drawl, baiting him. "With patience, an expert can enjoy a victim for years."

He flushes. "These shifters will not last years. You can't turn them, after all."

"As you say," I pretend to agree. "I suppose the shine wears off after a few weeks. Months, if the victim is special."

"Shifters are stronger than humans, but no one can withstand a vampire. They all break, in the end."

"Yes," I turn my attention back to the stage. "Everyone breaks in the end." Even vampires.

Minutes pass and I pretend not to notice the audience members studying me. I steeple my fingers. Tonight I will sit through the auction, feigning interest. In a month I will host a party with a select number of my lieutenants. By then I'll know which of my sired plotted against me. I already have an idea.

"Ladies and gentlemen, please take your seats. The final part of the auction is about to begin."

The house lights go down and a ripple of anticipation runs around the room. The curtain parts.

And she appears.

~

Selene

"Lot nine, special goods," the auctioneer announces.

I stand on the small platform, staring into an ocean of white light. The spotlights blind me before I remember to lower my gaze to the floor. I'm supposed to be submissive. A perfect little pet for a vampire.

"Female, wolf shifter, twenty-two. She has been trained in the submissive arts but..." the auctioneer pauses and lowers his voice. "She's never been blooded. Never been mounted either. That's right ladies and gentle vampires... she's a virgin."

Do I imagine an excited murmur in the rows beyond the lights? My training kicks in and smooths my features before my lip curls in disgust.

"Turn around, sweetheart, give us a show," the auctioneer orders.

I pivot dutifully, returning to my resting stance. I bow my head a little.

"Bidding starts at one hundred thousand," the auctioneer calls. "One hundred thousand for this pure, untouched virgin. Do I have one hundred—yes, there in the back. Gentleman in the red bowtie. Anyone else want to own this fine specimen of shifter beauty? Can I get two —" The bidding goes higher, spurred by the auctioneer's excited prattle. I squint into the lights. How many people are in the audience? Ten? Twenty? A hundred? Somewhere, perhaps in the balcony, Xavier watches.

It doesn't matter. I'm only here for one vampire, and one alone. Lucius Frangelico. I need to capture his interest.

I drop my gaze to the stage and try to look meek. What will entice a vampire king to bid on me? I lick my red lips, but can't bring myself to take a sultry pose. Not when I want to punch someone for subjecting shifters to this disgusting event.

My fists itch to clench. I force my shoulders to relax.

This will be over soon.

∼

Lucius

SHE'S NOT SUBMISSIVE.

That's my first impression of the beautiful she-wolf. She glares at the floor in front of her bare feet. Whenever the auctioneer mentions her virginal status, the corner of her mouth twitches. They dressed her in a soft bit of nothing, a garment closer to a negligee than evening wear. Something silky that begs to be ripped off. She has bruises on her arms—a sign she's been manhandled—but nothing about her is fragile. She's tall, tempting, an Amazon with a crown of white gold hair.

Something about her is familiar. She raises her head and shoots a glare into every corner of the theater, and the memory is lost. My body responds, blood rushing to my groin. What would it be like to own such a creature? To tame and master her?

I school my expression into one of boredom. The she-wolf tempts me, that's all. Something new and amusing to divert my attention for a time. Immortality reduces everything—pleasure and pain—into a temporary diversion. But this she-wolf might make me forget that for a little while.

On top of that, she looks like someone I once knew...

On stage, she licks her painted lips. My slacks grow tighter and my hands knot into fists. My bidding number rests on the floor next to my shoe. Dante must have left it there.

I won't bid tonight. But it is so tempting.

In the row in front of me, Theophilus clears his throat. "See what I mean, Sire?"

"Yes." I lean forward to study the she-wolf again. "I do."

Selene

"Five hunret, five hunret, can I get five hunret—" the auctioneer bleats as the auction runs out of steam. He pauses and scratches his chin. "No? Perhaps you need more incentive."

He waves to someone offstage and three beefy stagehands march straight towards me.

"What?" I mouth to the auctioneer, but he props an

elbow on the podium, settling in to watch. The first man reaches me and tugs at my dress' strap.

"Time to get naked, sweetheart."

My hand flies up before I can stop it. I push Mouth-breather Number One away from me as his two buddies arrive and clamp down on my arms, right on top of the bruises Xavier left.

"Bitch," Number One mutters. His beefy hand grabs the straps crossing over my back and tears them away. The garment sags, baring my breasts right as I get one arm free. My training kicks in. I lean left and kick the man on my right in the crotch. He goes down and I jerk, bringing the man on my left off balance. I smash my fist into his face and flip him over my back. He crashes into Number One. I crouch in a fighter's stance in the center of three downed thugs.

The auctioneer is laughing.

"Ladies and gentlemen, can I get a round of applause for lot nine?" A smattering of golf claps fills the theater. My cheeks heat. I didn't defend myself as part of some fucking act.

Except it was. Around me, the thugs stir and get to their feet. The auctioneer waves them off and they slouch away.

"Show's over, folks," the auctioneer announces. "Who wants to go home with her tonight? Bidding starts at five hundred thousand."

My dress tangles around my hips. I shove it off and kick it away.

"We've got a live one! Feisty. Will you be enough to master her? Five hundred and you'll find out."

Lucius

THE SHE-WOLF STANDS NAKED on stage, her chest heaving. Gone is any semblance of meek servitude. A lock of hair falls out of her braid and she tucks it impatiently away, glaring at everything and nothing.

She is magnificent. If I owned her, the fun I would have while we fought each other for dominance every night.

I'm not the only one who thinks this.

"Damn," Theophilus breathes. The next time the auctioneer calls for a bid, he raises his paddle. I bite back a snarl.

"Theophilus," I snap, putting enough compulsion in my voice to make his head snap around. I hold up my hand, palm up. "Give it to me."

He obeys, but all around me, vampires are bidding for the she-wolf. She stands in a pool of light, not even trying to hide her disgust. What made her agree to be auctioned? She's doesn't seem the type.

I beckon to Theophilus. "These shifters. If someone bids on them, do they get a portion of the money?"

Understanding lights his eyes. "No. They'll become your property. They don't come with anything. But their family might be compensated."

That matched the information I was given about the shifter slavers. These men, typically rogue shifters, found hidden shifter clans and offered money for the most submissive in the pack. Threats were also most likely involved. Would this she-wolf allow herself to be a part of such a bargain? Perhaps she agreed if the money went to her family.

I sit back as the bids rage around me. A mystery. I'm becoming more intrigued by the second.

"One million," someone calls a bid. I turn and look across the aisle. A large vampire wearing an eyepatch looks back at me. Only a lifetime of controlling my emotions keeps me from showing my surprise.

Xavier. What's he doing here? Our paths haven't crossed for decades. Maybe a century. He inclines his head in mocking acknowledgement. The last time we met, we were enemies.

There's quiet as the auctioneer and audience absorb his bid. Onstage, the she-wolf trembles as if she remembers why she's here.

And I remember who the wolf reminds me of. Her face becomes another, a waifish imp with a cloud of white gold hair. My first vampire lover. The only woman, perhaps, I ever loved. Georgianna.

Xavier's fangs glint at me from across the aisle. He never forgave me for taking Georgianna from him, and now he would snatch this wolf right from under my nose.

This one's mine, his gloating face seems to say. Poor she-wolf. Xavier always broke his toys. If not for fun, then to prevent anyone else from enjoying them.

My fingers clench on the bidding paddle. This whole auction, Xavier's appearance, the she-wolf who looks like Georgianna's ghost come to life—it's a ploy. A set up. It has to be. It's too convenient.

Somebody's up to something. If my sired have thrown their lots in with Xavier, then they have rebelled past the point of forgiveness. Their lives are over.

But if all of this is Xavier acting alone, then it might be interesting to play the game. Save the she-wolf. Parade her before my court, and draw Xavier into my net.

What is the saying? *Keep your friends close... and your enemies closer.*

Oh yes. These next few weeks will be very entertaining. I lean back in my seat and raise my paddle.

~

Selene

"One million."

Blood rushes to my head. That was Xavier's voice. He's bidding on me? Why?

I clench my hands in front of me, controlling my shudder. Have I failed? I can't fail. There's nothing left for me but the road ahead. The mission to entice Frangelico.

The silence stretches on and my nerves are screaming. Xavier doesn't like failure. That's a lesson I've learned over and over again. Pain is a great teacher. I'm strong enough to withstand it, but if I fail at this, I don't know—

A deep voice breaks the stillness. "Ten million."

A hush falls over the entire theater, every creature, me included, holding our breath.

The auctioneer looks like he can't believe his luck. "T-ten million." He mops his forehead and glances around the theater, biting his lip. I wait for him to raise the bid, but the staggering jump from one to ten million left him tongue-tied.

He raps his gavel and shouts. "Sold! To the gentleman with the deepest pockets. Vampire King Lucius Frangelico."

My ears ring. I stoop and gather up the pieces of the ripped dress. It worked. It worked! He bought me.

In a few minutes I'll be in the clutches of my new vampire master. Everything is going as planned.

The curtain sweeps across the stage, and I'm left blinking in the dark.

The auctioneer announces something about a break and walks off stage. Once he's in the wings, he beckons me to follow.

"Good girl." He rubs his hands together, probably imagining holding ten million dollars in his fat grubby fingers. I close my eyes, dizzy. What sort of vampire pays ten million for a wolf pet? What will he do with me?

It doesn't matter. It will all be over soon. Any bit of unpleasantness in the meantime, well, I've been trained to take a lot of pain.

Four guards march up and surround me. They don't touch me, so I don't make a fuss. Beyond them, the thugs who manhandled me lurk in the murky shadows. One has an ice pack to his face. The one who's crotch I hit is gone. The one left glowers at me, but doesn't get close. They won't dare touch me now. I belong to the Vampire King. The thought hits me like a blow and makes me sway on my feet.

A young, slender man appears at my elbow. I turn and

avert my eyes when I catch his scent. Not human. Vampire.

"His Majesty would like you to put this on." The young man holds up a suit jacket for me to slip into. I hand off my ripped dress to a guard and let the oversized jacket envelop me. The sleeves hang over my wrists and cover my legs to mid thigh. I've worn dresses that are less modest. I wore one tonight.

"His Majesty will collect you soon. Do you need anything? Food, some water?"

Shoes would be nice, but I shake my head. I tuck my face into the collar of the jacket and inhale the subtle, expensive cologne clinging to the fabric. The cologne doesn't hide the familiar cold stone scent. This jacket was recently worn by a vampire.

"This way." The auctioneer leads us into the green room.

The youthful vampire wrinkles his nose. "Do you expect the king to come back here? It's a dump." When the auctioneer grovels and denies that he would ever wish the great Frangelico to sully his shoes by stepping into this room, the young vampire growls, "Then find us a better place to wait. This is the king's property." He waves a hand at me. "The respect you show her is the respect you show the king."

That's how we end up in another room, smelling of fresh paint and filled with new furniture. It's upstairs. The young vampire fusses over me, finding me a bottle of water, and bemoaning my lack of shoes.

I tune everything out. Nothing matters until I meet Frangelico.

My new master.

No. He will never own me. He will think I belong to him. By the time he learns the truth, it will be too late.

I face the door and wait for the target to enter. Lucius Frangelico, the face that haunts me. The source of all my nightmares. The vampire who killed my pack, made me an orphan. If it wasn't for Xavier, I'd be dead. I owe him everything. And the debt will never be repaid. Xavier gave me life, but he also gave me a reason to live. Years of training and planning, culminating in a single mission: revenge.

And now I've been sold to the Vampire King. I will infiltrate his private home, let him bring me to his sleeping lair. Earn his trust. Wait until the moment is right.

All my life I've been waiting for this. All my training, all my hard work for one goal.

I'm going to kill Lucius Frangelico.

CHAPTER 2

ucius

THE CURTAIN FALLS and the house lights come up. I turn, but the aisle across from me is empty. Xavier is gone.

Pity. I would've liked to speak to him. We have a score to settle, going back hundreds of years. I doubt he's forgotten. A vampire never forgets.

Xavier will come to me again. I can feel it. We've only made our first moves in our little game.

Theophilus surges to his feet.

"Amazing, Sire," he gushes. "I have never seen anything like it."

I hand him my paddle and murmur instructions to him on how to complete my purchase. I give him my financier's card and send him off before signalling to my guards both seen and unseen. Four head to the stage to protect my recent purchase.

Vampires surround me, eager to congratulate me.

Dante appears at my elbow. "That was magnificent," he breathes.

"Your selection is exemplary," I say loud enough for all to hear. "You're to be commended."

Dante beams and I drop a heavy hand on his shoulder. "Get my purchase somewhere safe. See to her needs. When I come to collect her, there'd better not be a scratch on her, or whatever damage she sustains, I'll inflict ten times that on everyone in this place." I haven't forgotten the little ploy with the three thugs. Three thugs on one woman. She protected herself, but from now on she shouldn't have to. Keeping her safe is my responsibility and privilege.

Dante goes white. "Consider it done, Sire," he bobs his head. I grip his arm before he can dash off. "Wait." I shrug out of my suit jacket and hand it to him. "Put this on her." My scent will be enough of a deterrent to anyone who wants to harm her. A temporary mark of ownership until I give her one more permanent.

The one bright spot in this murky mess: I own the she-wolf now. I can do whatever I want with her.

I can hardly wait.

∽

Selene

. . .

The guards around me straighten a second before Frangelico walks in. He's tall, much taller than I am. His dark hair brushes the top of the door jamb. He's built like Xavier, but where my mentor's features are harsh and brutal, the Vampire King's are perfectly sculpted. I've seen sketches of him before from Xavier's surveillance, but nothing takes the edge off meeting him in person. Such a beautiful package to hold so much evil.

His eyes are dark, the color of coffee. He's swarthier than the drawings showed, his profile sharp and aquiline. His face belongs on a Roman coin, but more than that, his entire mien, look and build is that of an ancient king. For all we know, he was a king in his human days. An emperor. A conqueror.

My knees tremble, ready to kneel. I'm staring straight at him. He meets my gaze with a mocking quirk to his mouth.

Don't look him in the eyes. A tiny voice in my head screams. *Don't ever look vampires in the eyes.* With eye contact a vampire can control you. Of course, the older the vampire, the more powers they have. I bet Frangelico can control me with just a word.

I drop my gaze to his throat. His neck is large and masculine, framed by a white shirt collar. After you stake a vampire, you cut off its head and burn the remains, just to be safe. I've practiced countless times, first on dummies, then on real vampires—criminals Xavier caught and dragged to me for their death sentence. Staking and beheading and burning them was a rite of passage, meant to prepare me for this moment.

But now I'm here, faced with Frangelico, and all I can

think is "it would be a shame to destroy someone so beautiful."

I harden myself. This is the vampire who murdered my pack. Killed my entire family. Of course I'm going to kill him. In the end, it's either him or me.

A chill grips me. I shiver, and huddle deeper in the suit jacket I've been given.

Frangelico turns and murmurs something to a guard, who breaks from the pack and heads to the wall. To the thermostat.

That's when it hits me: Frangelico is in his shirt sleeves. I'm wearing his jacket. Breathing in his scent. I curl my bare toes into the carpet.

"Your Majesty, we are so honored you bid today." The vampire host steps forward. "And so delighted you won. And such a perfect lot to bid on. She is a prize."

Frangelico doesn't spare him a glance. "Is my car ready?" he asks the head guard.

"Yes, sir."

"You have use of this room as long as you like," the vampire interjects. "It's private. No one comes up here—"

"Leave us," Frangelico says.

The fawning vampire and the bodyguards exit without another word.

The Vampire King crosses the room and seats himself. I'm standing halfway between him and the window, twisting my fingers together. I've been trained to fight. This...is something different. The rules have changed. For the foreseeable future, this vampire is my master. He will command me and I will obey. Not unlike my relationship with my mentor, except...Xavier never made me feel this way. My insides are too hot, my skin too cold.

Xavier looked at me as project, a weapon to hone. And I am lethal. My beauty is my best weapon, but tonight it's turned against me. The Vampire King looks at me as a woman. His dark gaze strips me to the bone. Beyond naked, beyond vulnerable. I feel small and exposed, and thrillingly, wildly alive.

The Vampire King's beauty and appeal are his own weapons, and he deploys them well.

Frangelico raises a dark brow and goosebumps break out over my skin. My breathes rattles out of me.

Frangelico cocks his head slightly. "Pet?" His index finger points to the floor.

Right. Right.

I take a few steps towards him and lower myself into a kneeling position. Legs apart, palms facing up on my thighs. The suit jacket pools around me. I bite my lip. Should I have taken off the jacket?

I blink at the carpet.

"That's a good start," Frangelico sounds amused. "Now come closer."

I hesitate.

"You may rise. When you are in my home, you will crawl."

I duck my head. Get to my feet and go to stand at the spot where he's pointing. I keep my head down and resist the urge to fidget or shift.

Frangelico's voice is deep, a rolling baritone soothing my frayed nerves. "What's your name?"

"Selene." My voice wobbles.

"Selene," he repeats slowly, tasting every syllable. If he finds it strange that I don't have a last name, he doesn't mention it.

I suppress a shiver.

"A lovely name for a lovely pet. You may call me *Sir*."

My mouth parts but no sound comes out.

"They said you were trained."

It's not a question but I answer anyway. "Yes sir."

"Do you know this?" He signals, pointing two fingers to the floor in a V-shape.

In answer I rock my legs apart.

"Almost." Amusement tinges his voice. "Chin and chest up. Lock your hands behind your head."

I obey and the jacket falls open. My nipples are pointed straight at him.

"Cold, pet?"

I lick my lips before I answer. "A little." My voice is high and breathy.

Face thoughtful, he rolls up his sleeves, exposing strong forearms dusted with dark hair. My mouth goes dry. He motions for me to turn in a circle. I pivot, unsure at how much he can see while I'm wearing the jacket.

"This is your first time at auction?"

"Yes, sir." I blink at a spot above his head.

"You may look at me."

I obey without thinking. His eyes are twin dark pools; I fall in and drown.

"Such a beautiful wolf," he croons. "I will have to get you to shift for me. Soon. What color is your animal?"

I heave a breath. "White."

"Nervous?"

"Yes, sir."

"You needn't be," he murmurs. "I don't bite." Even as he says it his fangs flash. "Much."

My stomach flip flops and I fight to swallow.

Steepling his long fingers, Frangelico cocks his head to the left. "You haven't been touched?"

I shake my head. "No, sir."

Something flashes in his face. "Not blooded? Not even once?"

Throat too dry to answer, I shake my head.

He stands. I rock backwards, unable to keep from retreating. He's huge, taller than me by a fair amount, his shoulders broad as Xavier's. If he's thousands of years old, he must have been considered a giant when he was human. He looks down at me and I'm Alice in Wonderland, shrunk down. I'm a toy, a doll. I can only hope he doesn't break me.

A flash of white and I flinch.

"Easy, pet." He shows me the white handkerchief, amused again. It's easy to think other's fear is funny when you're the most powerful person in the room. I hold tight to my resentment as he gently rubs my lipstick away.

"There," he murmurs. "That's better." By the time he's done, the linen square is streaked with red. His scent envelops me and I lean closer, drinking it in. His cologne must be specially formulated to intoxicate a victim. I've never been this drawn to a vampire. Or any male, for that matter.

"Stay," he orders and moves around me. I should hate the way he orders me around like a dog, but I'm used to it. Most vampires treat shifters like dumb animals.

The Vampire King moves around me. Prickles go up my spine. The panicked voice in the back of my head warns me of a large predator behind me. I have to close my eyes and will myself to stand still. This is what Lucius bought and paid for: the right to touch me at will.

Long moments pass and he doesn't touch me. Finally—a soft tug on my head and a coil of hair falls. He's removing the pins in my hair, one by one. The braid comes undone, easing off my head and I sigh at the lessened weight. My hair cascades down my back, almost to my bottom. I rarely cut it.

Lucius' hand sifts through the thick tresses. Despite everything, the tension in my neck eases at his touch. He's petting me. I...don't hate it.

"Very good, pet," he murmurs. I raise my head. How long have I been standing here, letting him stroke my hair? Tingles spread through my body, anticipating those strong and gentle hands touching other parts of me.

Then he clamps a hand on the back of my neck and I go still. My pulse hammers under his thumb.

"You're doing well, pet. Someone has trained you. What I want to know is...who?"

My breath gusts out of me. Xavier and I concocted a story for this. Not far from the truth—not enough that anyone can tell I'm lying. "The vampires who took me from my pack. They taught me how to be a sweetblood."

"Interesting." His fingers reaffirm their grip. "Why did you join the auction?"

I gulp. "For the good of my pack." To avenge them.

"You allowed them to sell you?" His voice communicates disbelief.

"I went willingly, yes. I was sixteen."

"You've been in training this whole time?"

"Not to be a sweetblood. Not until I turned eighteen." I itch to turn and face him. "Before that, I was allowed to finish school. I was homeschooled."

"Sixteen years old." Frangelico muses. "And your pack let you go?"

"I was in foster care. My immediate family was dead." My voice is flat.

Frangelico drops his hand and steps away, returning to his seat. He signals and I obey, dropping to my knees beside his chair.

"My people are at this moment interrogating everyone involved in this auction. They will verify what you say. It's not that I don't believe you, but," he waves a hand. "I've been the target of more assassination attempts than I can count."

My blood runs cold. Does he suspect me?

"You needn't fear, pet. If everything checks out, no harm will come to you or your pack."

I stare at him. I know Xavier is smart enough to cover his tracks, but I hadn't guessed Frangelico would be so paranoid from the get go. I shouldn't be surprised. There's a reason he's still alive after hundreds, maybe thousands of years.

It's one thing to know that rationally. It's another to look into the eyes of an opponent who's stronger, faster, older and more knowledgeable than you, and make your next move.

One moment, Xavier told me. *One moment where he lets down his guard. That's all you need.* Just a few seconds and a stake. If I can make the killing blow, Xavier will find a way to make sure the Vampire King's organization is dismantled, their evil work finished for good. Xavier promised me that much. I just have to do my part, win Frangelico's trust long enough for him to give me an opportunity. What happens after is not my concern.

I never expected to come out of this mission alive.

Lucius toys with a lock of my hair, rubbing the silky strands between his fingers.

I take a deep breath. I should play the passive and meek submissive, but I can't stand to wait any longer. "Sir...may I ask...what are you going to do with me?"

He smiles and I quiver in response, a tuning fork plucked and playing a perfect note, just for him. "Why, pet, I'm so glad you asked." For the first time, he lays his hand against my cheek, touching my skin. My heart leaps into my throat as his dark eyes bore into me.

"First I'm going to take you home. Then, I'm going to make you mine."

I swallow hard. His thumb plays across my lips.

"Now." he sits back and signals. It takes me a moment to recognize the sign. I scoot back and go to all fours.

"Turn around," he murmurs and signals again. Slowly, I obey, crawling to face away from him and lowering my chest to the carpet. I rest my head on my arms. My hair pools around me, a white curtain I can hide behind. The suit jacket slides down my back, exposing my upraised ass.

His shoe nudges the inside of my right knee. "Wider, pet."

My entire backside is naked and vulnerable, and

pointed straight towards him. I've never felt more like chattel. Sucking in a breath, I wait.

His hand ghosts up the back of my thigh. Not touching but I can feel it there. My skin prickles in its wake.

Breathe, just breathe.

"Arch your back. Further. That's it." My entire backside tilts skyward. I'm a mannequin, a china doll, frozen in place, perfectly on display.

"Beautiful." Hot breath hits my nethers. My breath leaves my body. "So very beautiful. You're wet, Selene."

And I am. I press my lips together.

"Reach back and hold your bottom open," he orders, calm and casual as if remarking on the weather. "I want to see everything I own."

Eyes closed, I free my arms. Cheek to carpet, I put my hands on either ass cheek and expose myself further.

A slight touch between my labia makes me jump.

"Easy," he murmurs, gently stroking my wet slit. He circles my clit and I push slightly into his touch. Pleasure tightens, spiralling upwards. He takes his hand away and the sensation dissipates.

"No, pet. You have to earn that."

His finger touches my asshole, transferring the collected moisture. I whimper as he presses against the taut ring of muscle.

He chuckles. Takes his hand away.

He's sitting up. There's a rustle of cloth. I imagine him wiping his hand on his handkerchief.

I stay in place. I might as well be a statue he commissioned, carved from marble. Under the jacket, my skin is cold.

"You may rise."

I go to tall knees and he holds out his hand, helping me to my feet.

"You did well. I am looking forward to training you further."

My core muscles clench. *You're wet.* There's no reason I should respond this way.

Someone comes to the door and he eases away from me. I'm flushed and shaking. *Breathe, just breathe.* He's a vampire. There's nothing about him that should make me feel this way.

"Time to go, pet." Frangelico returns to me. He pulls out a leash and fastens it to my collar. His dark eyes flash. I hold my breath as we stare at each other. I can't bring myself to drop my eyes.

The corner of his mouth turns up.

He straightens and tugs. "Follow me."

We make it down the stairs an head for the back door. Guards in dark suits and sunglasses line the way, a mix of both mortal and vampire. My cheeks heat as I'm paraded in front of them, the barefoot subjugated slave. A pet on a leash.

We reach the door and Frangelico stops. A guard hands him something I don't quite see until the he turns and envelops me in its soft folds. A blanket.

My heart melts a little as he swaddles me.

The Vampire King wraps me up tight and picks me up, carrying me from the theater into the car.

∽

Lucius

WITH THE SHE-WOLF tucked into my arms, I settle into my seat. She looks a little dazed.

A guard shuts the door and she makes a little move. I tighten my hold.

"What is it, pet?"

"Shouldn't I kneel on the floor?"

"No. I want to hold you." I tip her back so her head rests on my arm. "Relax, pet. Sleep if you can."

"Yes, sir." When she's calm, her voice is low, soothing, a pleasing alto. When she's not, it gets high and breathy. Both pitches work dark magic on my body. I want to coddle her, treat her like a fragile flower. And I want to break her down and put her to her paces until she's blissed out and looking at me as her god. I want to do it over and over again.

Underneath my new pet, my cock threatens to burst from my pants. It's going to be a long car ride.

I check my phone as we glide through the night. My financier received my confirmation to transfer funds. Such an expensive little pet.

The she-wolf stiffens. I said that out loud.

"Don't worry." I tug her silky locks. "You're worth it."

In between petting her, I call Dante, ordering him to plan a massive party a month from tonight. To celebrate my new purchase. Dante falls over himself, promising to make it a night I'll remember. I smile at the double meaning, and hang up.

That's done then. I have one month to prepare for one

night. All of my sired are to be there. If they wish to stage a coup, that would be the night to do it. I'll be prepared. I'm always prepared. Caesar was a soldier, and trusted his men, but I'm a prince of Machiavelli's ilk. Better to be feared than loved. When I face my enemies, I don't just wound them. I destroy and scorch the earth.

"Sir?" Her meek voice pulls me from my thoughts. "Why did you do it?"

"Do what?" she should know better than to speak first, but I'll allow it. I'll enjoy breaking her bad habits.

"Bid on me." She gnaws her lip and I rest two fingers against her mouth to make her stop.

"You remind me of someone. A vampire. You have the same color hair." I remove my fingers and wipe them dry on the blanket. "I loved her once."

A furrow appears between her brows and I smooth it out.

"Oh yes, I can love."

"What happened?"

"She betrayed me," I answer. "Now, hush until I tell you you can speak."

Defiance flares in her eyes. There's my little fighter.

She sighs against my chest, her lower lip puffed out as she stares out the window.

"Now, now, don't sulk. Save your strength for the rest of the night. I promise you will need it."

A tremor goes through her.

"Close your eyes," I order. She slits them shut, but keeps squinting at the scenery. A little bit of rebellion. I will enjoy breaking her.

I won't fuck her, not right away. First I'll put her

through the paces until every move, every gesture and flick of her eyelashes pleases me. Some vampires would simply wipe their victim's minds and impress their will. I don't stoop to those tricks. Even my sired, once weaned from my blood, can choose to love me. My relationship with this wolf will be no different. She will rue and fear me, and I will teach her how pleasant it is to obey. I will bind her to me using every trick and technique I know. And in the end, I'll give her a choice: leave or stay. If she chooses to stay, she can be a sweetblood at my club. I'll never fuck or drink from her again. I cannot risk growing attached.

To love is to lose.

CHAPTER 3

S*elene*

THE VAMPIRE KING lives in a mansion high on a hill. It surprises me how elevated it is, on a pedestal in the Tucson foothills.

"Like it, pet?" Lucius' fingers massage my neck. I nod, remembering his speech restriction.

He chuckles. "Good girl."

I shouldn't like those words as much as I do. Lucius's presence affects me more than it should.

He's the enemy, I remind myself as he lifts and carries me into his house. Two men in dark glasses and unobtrusive earpieces open the double doors for us.

Frangelico swoops over the threshold and strides straight through the richly decorated house. I fidget a little in his arms, wanting to explore. My wolf doesn't feel safe in strange places.

Frangelico is determined to carry me.

"Do you want me to put you down, pet?" he murmurs, amused. I duck my head and he chuckles. "Are you so eager to crawl for me?" he whispers in my ear.

I flush as I remember what he told me. *When you are in my home, you will crawl.*

His laughter booms in his broad chest, reverberating through me. I'm not particularly small or delicate, but Lucius is well out of my weight class. And I'm supposed to submit to him.

So I relax and let him carry me through the high ceilinged chambers, through a bedroom with a king-sized four poster bed and into a bathroom big as a small house. I gape at the luxury as he sets me down on a tiled ledge next to a jacuzzi tub and crouches to start the water.

"A bath?" I mumble, shocked at the sight of the Vampire King on his knees, checking the temperature of bath water.

"Naughty pet, I told you not to speak."

I duck my head, waiting for a blow or some sort of retribution.

He just unwraps me and lowers me into the warm water. The temperature is perfect and I can't stop myself from relaxing and letting the water wash this sordid night away.

Lucius runs a finger down my shoulder, pausing to examine the bruises on my arm. "Did you fight your handlers before the auction?"

"No," I murmur. "But they weren't gentle."

A dark sound rumbles in Lucius' throat. He unwraps a

new bar of soap, but when I reach for it he holds it away. "Let me."

So I lie back and let the King of Vampires give me a bath. He scrubs every part of me with a soft cloth, including each finger. He has me face away from him and spends long minutes wetting and shampooing my hair. Each rinse washes away more of the intense events of the night. Selene the fighter fades into Selene the very pampered.

In all those years since Xavier came to my foster mother's home and explained to me why I was an orphan why I had no pack. He explained the murderer still walked free and clear and unpunished, and he offered me the chance for revenge. I left my foster mother and went into his care, a barracks a cold, stripped down soldier's life where pain and want were necessary tools to strengthen me. I spent the years between sixteen and twenty-one, those hormonal, formative years, learning to fight for my life every day, sleeping alone at night. Alone and untouched. Not even a mother's caress. Not even a pat on the back.

I didn't know how much I needed it, how much my skin missed human contact—even from someone who wasn't human—until now. Until Lucius Frangelico rolled up his sleeves and handled me. This powerful ruler kneeling for me, serving me.

He's not serving me, he's indulging himself. Asserting his rights. His hands move over my body, handling me like a ripe piece of fruit. Like an antique that's been hidden under layers of grime, found by a discerning eye and bought to be put on display. *You belong to me*, his fingers say. *You are now my possession.*

My body doesn't mind. It just wants more of his touch. Every inch of my body awakens under his large hands. My breasts swell, my nipples tighten. I should be planning my strategy and gathering my resources for a long, entrenched fight. Instead, I vibrate with nervous, expectant energy. What will he do next? Where will he touch me? How good will it feel? In just a few short minutes, he transforms me from a spy in his household, to a woman.

His hands trespass between my legs and I scissor them together. He just waits until I relax again, and slides his large fingers down the seam of my inner thigh. Sensation ripples through me. My lips part and I suck in air as he rubs the soap into the trimmed hair covering my pussy.

"Stand up." he orders, and signals me into the submissive position I took before, with my legs parted and my chest high, with my hands behind my head. "Eyes down."

I obey, but watch out of the corner of my eye as his shirt falls to the floor. He's stripping. I can't stop myself from looking up at the swarthy expanse of muscle. He's strong and perfectly formed, broad shoulders and tight stomach dusted with dark hair. A trail disappears into his trousers.

"Naughty pet." He tips my chin up. I hold his eyes until a soft swath of fabric settles over my eyes. He's using his tie to blindfold me.

"If you can't obey, you lose privileges," he murmurs, and there's an edge to his voice that makes my legs weak. He lifts me into position, setting me back on the ledge. "Now part your legs," he orders. I tremble for a few seconds before obeying.

"Hold still."

I go rigid as he soaps up the patch between my legs and shaves me. My abs tighten against panicked tremors at each pass of the blade, but my pussy throbs wildly.

"Perfect." Lucius runs a thumb over my smooth labia. A shot of water sluices across my sensitive bits as he takes the hand held sprayer and rinses me thoroughly. My hips tilt, seeking more stimulation.

His dark chuckle fills the bathroom.

Still blindfolded, I am rinsed and dried and swaddled in a fluffy robe. I reach for the eye covering and get a light nipple tweak in chastisement. He makes me wait a few minutes before removing it. He changed into a dressing robe, tied loosely over his broad chest and black slacks. He's barefoot, but no less intimidating.

"Hungry, pet?" he asks, and lifts me in his strong arms before I can answer. Apparently he's going to carry me everywhere tonight. I like it way too much. I'd rather he throw me in a dungeon, chain me up and feed me bread and water. Based on Xavier's training, I expected to be brought into the enemy's lair, beaten and subjugated and punished. I never expected to be pampered. I don't have any defenses against kindness.

My body alive and singing, he carries me to the kitchen and seats me at a table.

He sets a plate down in front of me. Simple fare. Bread, cheese, a few rosettes of prosciutto and olives. Antipasti.

He gestures to the plate with a log of salami. "Eat, little wolf."

I take a few bites, watching him as he unwraps the stick of meat and takes a bite.

I drop the olive meant for my mouth.

"What is it, Selene?"

"You're eating," I point out dumbly.

"I can eat and drink as you do." He looks pointedly at my plate until I retrieve the fallen olive and pop it in my mouth. "I just do not need to."

"But I thought…" I flush.

"You thought I'd be dining on you?"

I stare at my plate, no longer hungry.

"I will one day. When you are trained. You will beg for it."

"What? No," I say before I can stop myself.

"You think you can withstand me?" He picks up a napkin and wipes his large hands, smiling. Even sitting, he's head and shoulders taller than me. I feel like a child at a giant's table. He could just manhandle me into doing whatever he wants. Did I really think my training would make me his equal?

"Speak, pet. Tell me what you fear."

"Are you going to wipe my mind?" I ask what's been bothering me. Xavier said Frangelico wouldn't stoop to such measures, but it's possible. He could make me forget everything. Replace my memories with whatever lies he wanted.

"I don't want a mindless puppet. If I did, I wouldn't have bid on you."

The promise of a vampire is worthless, but you can bet on their pride. I believe Frangelico. He wants a pet to willingly bow to him. He'll train me the way he wants, and present me to his vampire subjects at the party he's planning.

"Ten million dollars," I say. "What makes you think I'm worth it?"

He tosses the napkin onto his plate. "I've already gotten my money's worth. You're a fighter. Unwilling to be cowed. You fake submission when it suits you."

I hold still, trying not to twitch. Frangelico's in my head. *No, he's just observant.* Two thousand years of studying human behavior. Did I think I would fool him so easily?

The question is: how long do I have before he figures out the reason I'm here? And when he does, how long will I survive?

My heart flutters in my chest, a bird in a snare struggling to be free. The Vampire King seems to know how he affects me. Worse, he enjoys it.

He leans forward. "But I'll tell you something, pet, something you won't even admit to yourself. Underneath, you want to submit. You fight that most of all."

A rush of adrenaline almost has me bounding out of my seat. I hit the table with my fist, glowering at Lucius.

"No. You're wrong."

Lucius

I'M SO RIGHT.

Ah, delicious. So much fight. She's nothing like Georgianna, who was a meek thing, willing to please. Selene is a cooling zephyr in a desert. I enjoy riling her up as much as I enjoy putting her in her place.

I tilt my head to the side. "Care to wager?"

"What?"

"Let's play a game, pet. I will do everything I can to elicit your submission. You will fight me. One hour." I raise a finger. "It is up to you to resist me, and me to convince you to submit."

"You could just hurt me until I break," she points out.

"I could. But I will not. Tonight I will not hurt you...much."

"That's not very reassuring."

"Life rarely gives us reassurances. But I will give you one: you will experience as much pleasure as you do pain. Perhaps more." I pause and let my voice deepen. "A lot more."

She runs a finger around the edge of her plate, considering.

"What do you say, pet? My skill against your will."

"How do we know who wins?"

"I'll let you decide. Only you can know if you've truly surrendered."

Her brow furrows. "You could just compel me."

"That's cheating." She gives me a look, and I suppress a laugh. "How about this? I swear on my grave I will not compel you. Ever."

"Ever?"

"I keep my promises, pet. Now you have no reason to hesitate."

But she does, so tense I remind her to breathe.

"It's just a harmless little game," I soothe. "I have so

little entertainment these days. You could prove, once and for all, that you have the will to stop me. Or I could prove that deep down, you want me to take control. One hour. One night. May the best one win."

A little quiver goes through her. Very good. She's knows the risks of playing with a vampire. Still, she's curious. I smell it in her scent.

"What will you give me if I win?"

"Whatever you want."

Her eyebrows shoot up. "And if I want to leave?"

"Do you want to leave? Where would you go? Another vampire might snap you up, especially after that show on the stage. They're watching you and I, even now. If you walk out of here, they won't hesitate to grab you, and bend you to their will, if only to prove that they can cow you better than I." Fear flares in her scent and I finish, "You're safer here with me, the King of the Vampires, than with anyone else."

She blows out a breath. She knows I'm right.

"Is there anything else you desire?" I ask.

"Crawling. I don't want to crawl." Her mouth is set in a grim line. "You said I would have to crawl when we're at home."

"Very well, pet. If you win, you will only crawl if you desire it."

Her chin jerks up. "I won't ever desire it."

I just smile.

Selene

. . .

The Vampire King smiles and my bones melt. I steel myself for an attack, but it never comes. Only these subtle games that keep me guessing.

"Finished?" He indicates my plate. I nod and he comes around to help me out of my chair. *Predator,* my body screams when he steps behind me. I half rise before he pulls my chair away. He offers his hand and I hesitate. His look turns mocking. I'm not scared of holding his hand, am I?

Of course I am. But I won't let a little thing like fear stop me. Lucius proposed this game, and I'm going to win. At worst, I'll learn more about what he's about. At best, I'll prove he'll never be my master.

He leads me into a long room that ends in french doors overlooking a dark patio. Chairs and coffee tables and couches, a gorgeous bar, paintings on the wall—everything is pure, opulent but tasteful luxury. In between two windows is a long expanse of wall covered by a tapestry. Lucius positions me in front of it and draws the cloth hanging aside, exposing two large wooden bars set in an X formation.

"Are you familiar with the St. Andrew's cross?" Lucius bends to open an antique looking chest. "The saint was crucified on a diagonally shaped cross. Upside down, by his request. Don't worry, pet. We won't be reenacting that particular scene."

I shiver but stay where he put me. He strips off his dressing robe, baring his chest again before approaching me. I expect him to strip me roughly, but he only gathers my hair back. He fiddles with it for a moment. What is he doing? He's not...no way.

Lucius Frangelico, Vampire King, is braiding my hair.

When he's done, he steps back and looks me up and down. He must like what he sees, because he turns away with the order, "Strip and stand in front of the cross, facing outwards."

The game has begun, and it's a mind fuck. I'm supposed to participate willingly in my subjugation.

This doesn't mean I submit to him, I tell myself as I undo the tie on the robe and let it fall. If I let him put me on the cross, I know what will happen. He'll use an implement on me—some medieval torture device he keeps in the trunk by the window—and it'll hurt.

But I can take the pain.

After the soft touches that confuse me, I'll welcome it. I need to remember to hate Lucius Frangelico.

I can't suppress a tremor as he returns to my side. He takes my wrists and secures them above my head in cuffs attached to the cross, and kneels to loosely bind my feet apart. His dark hair brushes my thigh and my heart nearly pounds out of my chest.

"Breathe, Selene," he murmurs. "Don't forget to breathe."

I obey, taking big gulps of air. This is going to hurt, but I'm ready. Xavier made sure I could withstand discomfort and pain, all sorts of pain. I lay awake long nights, my body aching, wondering what tortures Lucius might choose to inflict on me. I can endure anything when I focus on Lucius' death. I close my eyes and imaging the killing blow.

"Comfortable?" He jars me out of my concentration. He has me wiggle my fingers and toes, checking that the bonds aren't too tight. I want to glare at him. What's his game? If you tie a woman up to hurt her, what does it matter if her circulation is good? Keeps her alive longer, I guess. I wouldn't expect a vampire to care.

"A few rules." He moves out of my line of sight. "I'm in charge of the scene, but you can stop it at anytime. Just say, *Stop*. If I've gagged you or you can't talk, snapping your fingers means the same thing. Nod if you understand."

I bob my head, but I still don't get it. He won't stop if he doesn't want to. Would he?

Lucius takes his place in front of me. "This is a flogger." He shows me his chosen tool. Black strands hang from a smooth mahogany handle. He runs the flogger up and down my body and I shiver.

"No need to fear. I can make it feel good." He flicks his wrist and flogs my chest. The strands fall in a light rain.

"Does that hurt?"

I jerk my head to the left.

"Answer me. You can speak out loud. Does this hurt?" He repeats the movement.

"No."

He raises a brow.

"I mean, no, Sir."

"Good. How about this?"

He swings his arm, flogging me in a criss cross motion. The strands hit my skin with a harder thud. I register the impact but again, it's miles away from pain.

"No," I sigh.

"That's it, pet. Just enjoy it. Think of it as a massage. Sensation."

I blow out a breath and my shoulders move away from my ears.

"That's it. Relax." Lucius' voice deepens. He's one hundred percent focused on me, his movements slow and controlled. The flogger is an extension of his large body. He whips my chest until my breasts are pink. The flogger dances down my body, slapping my hips and thighs, coming close to my pussy without trespassing. I rock my weight from left to right in subtle response to each soft impact. Heat dances through my body, lulling me into compliance.

"Let's make this a little more interesting," Lucius says. He disappears and returns with a small wooden chest. I crane my neck but can't see past the open lid until he removes what he wants, puts the chest away and shows me two tiny rubber and metal clamps.

"Uh-uh," I shake my head and he makes a show of waiting. I don't say *stop*, but I glare at him while he attaches the clamps to my nipples. A slight pinch, but my pussy pulses in sympathy. My breasts swell as if happy for the attention.

"Now." Lucius shakes out the flogger, and whips up and down my legs, warming them up, painting them pink. A few sharp snaps leave red lines on my thighs but no expected bloom of pain. Nipples throbbing, I greet the flogger's rough kiss eagerly.

"You like this?"

I'm breathing hard, the bloom of arousal growing.

Lucius leans over me, covering me with his powerful body, and my very skin leaps at the thought of him touching me. I turn my face up to accept a kiss, but he pushes the flogger between my legs and rubs there.

"How about this? Do you like it?" Before I can answer in the negative, he holds the flogger up in front of my face. "Don't lie to me."

I can see as well as he can: the strands are wet.

"That doesn't mean anything," I growl.

"Of course it doesn't. Your body is beautiful, and it's a natural reaction. Just let yourself go, Selene."

I growl to myself. He's only in charge if I allow it.

As if he reads my thoughts, he steps forward and releases both nipple clamps at the same time. Pain shoots through me and detonates in my pussy. I sag in my cuffs.

"Hmmm," he murmurs, sounding pleased. I stiffen my legs and stand straight. A little pain won't best me.

A smile plays on his lip as if he gets my unspoken message, and thinks it's cute. He studies me carefully, checking me over.

"You ready to turn around? I'll work your back harder," he warns.

I raise my chin. "Do your worst."

Smiling to himself, he unties me and flips me around. "From here on out, I'm calling the shots." He steadies me, moving my arms and legs where he wants them. Again he tests my fingers and toes, making sure I have good circulation. He tucks my braid over one shoulder.

"You have a gorgeous ass," he tells me, running his hand down my back and flank, stopping to grab a handful. "So tight and plump and delicious. I can't wait to fuck it."

With that little promise sapping the strength from my knees, he steps back and dusts my back with the flogger.

I press my forehead against the wood and relax into the rhythm. Left, right. Left right. Blood pumps, my breath flows in and out. Heat creeps over my back and ass. Lucius spends particular time flogging my butt until it's warm to touch. Still no pain.

"I wonder," he murmurs and snaps his implement so the ends bite between my shoulder blades. A sharp sting that fades almost as quickly as it came. Heat floods through my core.

"No," I blurt, in response to my building arousal.

"No?" Lucius asks. "Do you mean *stop*?"

My safeword. He's testing me.

I shake my head. "Keep going."

He makes a cluck of disapproval. "Are you in charge?"

"No, sir." I attempt to sound meek.

He makes a growly sound in his throat that makes my wolf shiver with ingrained submission, but he does return to flogging.

I grab the ties binding my wrists and hold on. Lucius lets himself off his self-imposed leash, flogging me with greater and greater fervor until I've pushed up to tiptoe. I'm not sure if I'm trying to get away from the lash, or trying to give him more skin to strike. My body is one long, smooth line secured to the cross, the blush moving across my body like a rose coming to bloom. I close my eyes and bow my head, still gripping the bindings tight. Behind me a harsh inhale, a grunt followed by the delicious snap are the only proof I'm not alone. I imagine Lucius' body leaning into the strikes, shoulders flexing, forearm hard as iron, face composed. I wish I could see him.

I wish I could rub my pussy on this polished wood. Every stroke carries me higher. The flogging continues, and I don't know when it happened, but suddenly I'm floating. I'm floating in a warm, pink patch of air.

"You're doing so well, Selene." The flogger's smooth handle touches my labia's soft folds, followed by his fingers. I whimper.

"You're so wet. So delicious. A juicy peach, I could just eat you." I flinch and he laughs. "Maybe later. Right now, this is all I want." He keeps rubbing and I twist out of reach.

"What are you doing?"

His arm snakes around, securing me so he can keep fondling me. He sets his chin on my shoulder and murmurs in my ear, "Does it feel good?"

My chest heaves as my orgasm floats closer.

"Ask me permission before you come."

I shake my head no, more for my own determination than response to him. No, I will not ask permission. No, I will not come.

"All right." He steps away and I sag forward, my body bowing at the loss. He wipes wet fingers on my ass before taking his spot behind me. The flogger flies again, stinging my back with the soft leather strands.

"It's your choice, pet. Always your choice."

How can that be true? How did I end up here, tied up willingly, dying for touch, sensation, anything. A soft touch. A stinging rain. Anything.

"You're a strong woman." The flogger thuds up and

down my back. "You want to prove it. I understand. But, Selene"—He pauses to step close and trail the strands over my ass until tingles run up my spine—"there's nothing wrong with letting go. You want it." His voice deepens, darkens. "I want it. In bondage, you can fly free."

I don't know what the hell he's talking about. I lean on the cross, hanging from the cuffs, my fingers fondling my chains. I want to arch my back and rub my pussy against this wood. I want to push my ass backwards and beg him to flog me harder.

"Harder," I whisper to the wood grain.

"What's that, Selene? What do you want?"

"Harder. More."

"Good girl." He rewards me, warming me up with every increasing blow. I twist and dance as the beat on my back pushes me higher.

∼

Lucius

My pet's back is a pretty pink painting, slashed through with red. She responded better than I could have dreamed, enjoying the warm up and willing to go to the next level. I crouch to inspect a particularly cruel mark on her ass. Her shifter healing is kicking in, flooding her body with endorphins. As I rise, I get a whiff of her juicy cunt.

I set aside the flogger and do what I've been longing to do all night. I run my hands over her body, soothing and claiming her heated flesh.

"Ooooh," she sighs into my touch. She's been longing for it, too.

I'm not all gracious. I squeeze and pinch and admire my marks. "You wear my marks so well, pet. I should whip you every night."

She shivers but the wet folds of her pussy tell me how she really feels.

"You've been such a good girl," I whisper. "I'm going to touch you now and let you come. You'll have to ask nicely when you're on the edge." I press my body against hers, clamping my left arm around her narrow waist and reaching between her legs with my right. She's so wet, my fingers are soaked by the time I find her clit and nudge the sensitive spot along its side. She's right on the edge, pressing against my hold, breath gusting. I hold her tighter.

"Ask for permission," I order.

She tosses her head, still proud, but when I touch her again, she melts. I rub faster, taking note of her flushed chest, her harsh breathing. She's done so well, I want to reward her. But first—

"Ask, Selene."

"Please—"

Yes. "Come for me," I growl in her ear and nip her soft lobe. Her body shudders, bucking and responding. She cries out as she tips over.

Magnificent.

"That's it, baby," I croon and hold her close. I let her come down and sag against the wooden frame. She worked hard for that one. One day I'll work her up and over again and again, all night. But not tonight. We're done.

I uncuff her and let her down, gathering her up in my

arms. I carry her to my giant leather chesterfield, set facing the cross for this purpose. A water bottle and small towel waits on a side table. I open the water and dribble a little into her mouth before wetting the washcloth and wiping her down. I give her the rest of the water, holding the bottle for her, and wrap her in a soft blanket. Her cheeks are flushed, her lips plump and begging for a kiss. For a bite.

Not tonight. I run my tongue over my fangs once, and settle into the huge armchair with my boneless armful.

"You're so beautiful." I tell her. "You did so well. Very good, very good."

She gives a happy sigh.

After a few minutes, I sit up and reach for the mini fridge next to the chair. It holds juice and chocolate, everything necessary for aftercare. I feed her from my fingers. She drinks deeply, her dark eyelashes fluttering.

When she's done, I tip her back in my arms. Her braid has come undone and I take a moment to spread the fine spun silk over her shoulders. After a moment she snuggles in with another sigh. I remember her confusion as I checked her circulation and gave her a safeword.

"You've never done this before, have you? You may answer me," I add, in case she remembers the speech restrictions I put on her earlier.

She licks her lips. "Taken orders from a master? I was trained…"

I interrupt her story. "But they didn't care for you, not like this."

"No." She looks uncertain. Her body should be singing with endorphins and submissive desires. Her mind appears to be whirring, wondering what happens next. She's confused, maybe a little disturbed.

I tuck her closer to me and stroke her neck through her hair until she sighs.

"I'll ask many things from you, pet. Your submission. Your obedience. Your fear." A little tremor goes through her and I knead the back of her neck, soothing it away. "But most of all…" I turn my head and whisper right in her waiting ear, "I want your thoughts. All of them. You don't need to worry about pleasing me. I will tell you what to do, and you will obey. I will bear every burden, every worry. All I ask is you obey me. You can have everything you want, pet, if you submit to me. There's a whole world of pleasure for us to explore, and I will be your guide. I can lead you to the heights of ecstasy, and carry you safely home."

Another sigh at that, but her brow furrows. I smooth the lines there with a finger. "Stop thinking. Just be."

My speech earns me a few whole minutes of silence. I enjoy the soft, breathing bundle in my arms. My pet is the most delightful mix of contradictions. One minute fighting, the next using her powerful will and strength to submit. A virgin come boldly to learn the arts of Venus. She should provide long months of entertainment, if I don't break her.

When she's ready to sit up, I let her, but keep my arms around her.

She squints at me. "Do you do this a lot? Train a submissive?"

"No. I have a club of submissives but they are already

trained. Most come knowing how to please me. The only submissive I trained myself was…" I stop.

She guesses why. "The one you loved?"

"She came to me eager to please. Unlike some I know."

With shocking cheek, she rolls her eyes. My laugh surprises us both.

∿

Selene

THE VAMPIRE KING has a lovely laugh. His whole face lights up, all the sharpness of his beautiful features softening. The deep chuckle that rolls out from his chest ripples through my body, easing the tightness shaken loose by the joyful earthquake. Warmth curls through me, waking up secret places. I can't stop responding to him.

"Ten million buys a lot of obedience," Lucius says with a smile that does things to me. "There's not an obedient bone in your body. But you'll learn how pleasing it can be."

I wrinkle my nose at that, and he laughs again.

"I don't think I've laughed this much in…" He stops to think. "I can't remember."

"I'm glad I amuse you," I say in a dry tone.

"You are the most delightful pet," he pronounces.

Ugh, I hate him calling me that.

"I'm going to take of one final thing, and then you're going to bed. Alone," he clarifies. "To rest."

"That's it? We're done for the night?" I wriggle my bottom on his lap. His arms clamp tighter, but not before I get a rise out of him. Literally.

He pauses to drown me in those coffee black eyes before saying, "Careful, Selene. The monster will awaken in its own due time. No need to rouse him early."

"I think he's already awake," I quip. Seems a bit weird to call your cock a 'monster' but okay.

Lucius fists a large hand in my hair, holding me still. "Careful," he warns, but he's smiling. "I am already tempted to push you to the limits of ecstasy, and use your body in all the ways it begs to be used."

The shot of arousal in my scent seems to surprise us both.

"But," Lucius enunciates with raised finger, "You are young. A virgin. In many ways, a beginner."

I open my mouth to protest—I'm curious now about all this ecstasy he's promised—and he stuffs two fingers in my mouth. Robbing me of the ability to speak.

"You will learn, pet. It will be a delight to teach you."

In a movement too quick to follow, he pulls out his fingers, wipes them on the blanket, catches my chin and holds my face. His wicked smile makes me weak. I part my lips, ready for him to claim my mouth, but he kisses my brow.

"Now. There's a matter of your punishment. I told you earlier not to speak." He tips me over his knee. I land hands on the ground.

"That's it. Like that."

My feet kick and he clamps a leg over my knees. His hand smacks my ass and I yelp, more pissed than in pain.

The spanking continues with rapid fire swats. The sting crashes around me. Like with the flogging, it's not altogether unpleasant, especially once the initial sting turns to heat. All at once, he stops and rubs my bottom, and the ache fades away, turning into that high flying feeling.

"Magnificent, pet," he growls. His finger delves under me, finding sensitive points. Pinning me when I struggle. He's going to rip my orgasm from me and I don't know whether I'm squirming to fight it off, or urge it to come faster.

"You're going to stop worrying." He whispers as he frigs my poor clit. "You don't have to wonder whether or not you please me. I'll tell you. From now on, you simply *be*. Do as I say and all will be well." His voice comes from far away. "Let it go. Now."

I break, gasping. Lucius drives his fingers into my sopping pussy, pushing me higher. We've known each other less than a night and he knows just how to touch me.

The room tilts, and I'm in his arms again. The pleasure, the pain, the events of the night and rioting sensations ride through me, carrying my sated body into unconsciousness. I fall asleep with him crooning, "Good girl."

CHAPTER 4

Selene

A BAND of sunlight falls across my face. I kick my legs, frantically freeing myself from the sheets. I'm in a strange room, in a strange bed. I sit up and the pieces fall together: the auction. The ten million dollar bid. The King of the Vampires bought me and now I'm in his home.

Scariest of all: I slept like a baby. No dreams, no nightmares. No waking to check for monsters in my room. I haven't slept this well since I was eleven, freshly orphaned. That's when I learned the monsters were real.

I had the best sleep of my life in my vampire enemy's home. Worse, I fell asleep in his arms. Around Lucius, my body loses all good sense.

I roll my heavy limbs out of bed and do a few stretches before prowling around the luxurious bedroom.

Door locked. Of course. I'm a captive here. Lucius is

smart enough to know ten million dollars doesn't make me a willing possession.

I head to the bathroom to do my business. The room is sunny thanks to a row of high windows near the ceiling. I could break out if I wanted to, but my mission is far from complete.

Once you are inside his house, you must be doubly vigilant, Xavier told me. *Vampires do not let their guard down when they bring someone close to their lair. Frangelico's place of rest will be well protected.*

Then how will I get close enough to kill him? I asked Xavier. Before he answered, he smiled so wide his fangs flashed at me.

I splash water on my face and drink from the tap. Today I rest, explore and prepare myself as best I can. Tonight the real work begins.

For now I'm alone. Vampires sleep during the day. Lucius might send a servant to care for me, but until then, I'll conserve my strength the best way I know how.

Going to all fours, I stretch and shift into my wolf. Bright smells burst in my brain, my wolf nose telling me what scents make up this vampire bouquet. Lucius has his house cleaned regularly. The perfumed cleaner his housekeeper uses makes me sneeze. Other than someone entering to clean, this room has been unused for a long time, but still holds the scent of vampire.

I sniff around the room's perimeter. By the time I make it to the door, voices outside make me retreat to the foot of the bed. I fluff my fur and display my teeth to look as big and mean as possible. As werewolves go, I'm of average size, bigger than a normal wolf. In human form I'm deadly to vampires, but my wolf is better suited to fight out of a tight space.

Three people are standing in the hall, arguing. A hand grabs the door handle, then undoes the lock.

He spots me right away and grins. "Well, hello, wee wolfie."

Teeth bared, I stand my ground. Two more heads pop around the door to peer at me. One is wearing a fedora over grey hair, the other is taller with giant prescription glasses. They smell like shifters, but I can't place their animals. A growl escapes my throat and the dark haired one raises his hands like I've drawn a gun.

"Easy, we're just here to check on ya. Don't bite the messenger." His Irish brogue tickles my ears. "We're here to check on ya."

Someone must have elbowed him in the side because he grimaces and starts struggling. "Lay off."

"Tell her Frangelico sent us—" the tall one with big glasses murmurs.

"I'm tryin'!"

"Well, do it before she eats us—"

The three crash to the ground, pushing at each other and cursing. Their scent is a confusing tangle of werewolf, feathers, and Irish whiskey. My nose twitches but I can't help grinning at their antics. The dark haired one pushes up first, struggling to his knees while his buddies sprawl around him. The gawky one's glasses hang from one ear and the grey-haired one has lost his fedora.

"I'm Declan," the Irish one announces. "Frangelico ordered us to check on ya. Give ya food and water, that sorta thing." He looks around and grabs the fedora right before the grey-haired guy can get it. "The rest of these ijits can introduce themselves. I'm the handsome one."

"I'm Parker," the grey haired guy rises and dusts himself off. He snatches the hat back and hands it to the tall one.

"L-l-laurie," stammers the tall guy who smells like feathers.

"I've never been in a vampire's house before," Declan remarks. "Do ya think we should explore?"

"No!" both Parker and Laurie yell.

"Jay-sus, no need to shout. I'm not deaf, ya know." Declan sticks a finger in his ear and twists it around. "What say ya, wolfie? Ready to get some fresh air?"

I assess them a second. Three shifters, unknown animals. Close friends, somehow working for Frangelico. Threat level: zero.

I bark once. When they head out of the room, I follow.

For never being in Frangelico's house before, they seem to know their way to the kitchen. The three knot together for a whispered conference.

"Is she staying in wolf form? Should we just go with it?"

"I guess...Just act natural."

Parker pours fruit out of a bowl and fills it with water. He sets it down for me while Declan opens the fridge.

"What do you want? Steak?" The Irishman holds up one finger, "or lasagna?" he holds up a second. I bark once.

"Good choice." He lays out my steak on a platter, sets it on the floor and backs away. The three lean on the counter at the far end of the kitchen while I rip into my breakfast.

They talk amongst themselves, slowly growing bolder. How did these guys end up working for the Vampire King? They're wondering the same thing about me.

After breakfast, they let me outside, and I roam around do my business on the base of a saguaro cactus. I sniff around a palo verde tree. I'm careful to stay away from the jumping cactus.

I spend the rest of the morning lazing on the warm patio, napping and gnawing on the steak bone that one of my sitters left out for me. I act like a normal canine pet, all the while clocking the guards' patrol times, and the location of the security cameras set around the estate.

Around noon, someone comes to the front door. Declan and Parker's surprised voices echo through the house. They accept the packages, and carry them—box after box full of shopping bags—down the hall towards my room.

Declan pops out to check on me a few minutes later. "Frangelico, uh, ordered you some things. Must've had three personal shoppers working round the clock for ya. Clothes, make up and, er…" He flushes and I have no trouble guessing that a good portion of the bags came from a high end lingerie company. "We, um, left them in your room. We'll let you unpack them."

I nod and go back to worrying my bone.

The Irish wolf squats down a few feet away.

"Frangelico wants us to find out what happened to your pack. Do ya have any clues ya can give us, lass? Any leads?"

What? Why would Frangelico order these guys to find my pack? What is he trying to prove?

He said he'd check my story. What will he do when he finds out who I am? That I'm the only wolf who got away?

Declan scratches his head, as if wondering how I'm going to communicate to him in wolf form. There's no way I'm telling him anything so I stare at him until he looks away.

"Right," he says, and goes back inside.

I doze for a few hours before they call me inside for dinner. Salmon this time.

"Here wolfie, wolfie, wolfie," Parker pours a bottle of fancy Fiji water into my clean bowl. Nothing but the best for the vampire king's pet.

At 3:00 p.m, the trio tries to lure me to my room with dog treats. I play along and let them lock me back in my room. They didn't ask to be my keepers. My problem isn't with them. I've got a few hours left before I face Frangelico again, and I need my wits sharp as a wooden stake. As the light in the bedroom thickens and turns amber, I change into human form and curl up in the bed to sleep.

I wake at sunset. Somehow I know. I take a shower, dry my hair. Use the primping tools. I'm not the best at doing my hair but I manage to tame it. Frangelico seems to prefer a natural look, so other than chapstick, I leave off the makeup. I sift through several hanging dresses and about thirty shopping bags, finally selecting a flirty little romper with a V neck of scalloped lace. No shoes, no bra, just a tiny thong. White. I'm still a virgin, after all, and I'm not going to let the vampire forget.

Finally, I stand in front of the door, combing my fingers through my hair so it falls in sexy waves around my shoulders. I pinch my cheeks and bite my lips, but thinking about what Lucius might do to me tonight has my color high.

My plan is simple. I'm in Lucius' house, but I haven't yet penetrated his defenses. I'll never get a chance to strike if he doesn't let me in. I have to earn his trust, and that means using all the weapons at my disposal. My beauty, my body, my submission.

I have to seduce him.

About an hour after sunset, my door clicks. I wait, but no one enters. When I check the door, I find it's been unlocked remotely. I open it wide and consider the dark hallway.

Somehow, I know he's waiting for me. I bet anything there's a camera on my door, not to mention in my room.

Before I take a step, I remember what he said last night and sigh inwardly. This is a test. It's a lot like living in Xavier's military compound. Everything is a test and any gift comes with a high price. I promised Lucius my submission, and I'm going to give it to him. I'll be his perfect little pet until the last, when I turn on him and shove my submission so far down his throat he chokes.

With that savage thought warming my insides, I drop to all fours and crawl.

∼

Lucius

. . .

I HOLD my breath as Selene's white blond head appears. I set aside my tablet with the feed from the security cameras seconds before she rounded the corner. She stood in the doorway of her room so long I was about to go and get her. Then, in a movement so graceful it squeezed my heart—and my cock—she stretched out on her hands and knees. Kneeling for me. Crawling for me. I've never been tempted to permanently collar a submissive, but this she-wolf is a perfect mix of defiance and willingness to please. It's easy to imagine long nights together, her stretched out before me, quivering flesh caressed by firelight, waiting for my bite. She'd be mine. All mine.

As she crawls closer, hips swaying, her eyes flash up at me. I meet her gaze with brow raised, and she ducks her head, then frowns at her natural reaction to my dominance. For all her insistence that she's been trained by vampires, she's not used to being the least dominant predator in the room.

She's gnawing her lip. I'll have to put a stop to that particular habit. The only one who gets to bite her is me.

I beckon her closer. She crawls well, slinking across the floor like a cat but her back should arch more to best display her face and ass. I'll have her practice later, as part of her training. It'll be a pleasure to teach her.

She settles in front of me, between my feet, her blonde head bowed, hands upturned on her bare thighs. The romper she chose slouches over her bare breasts. When I lean forward, I can see all the way down to her bare nipples.

"Excellent, pet." I settle my hand around her neck, enjoying her quiver, and position her on all fours in front of me. I run a hand down her spine, pressing on her lower back until her ass cants upward. "Look at me," I murmur.

She blinks at me. Her face is free of makeup and exquisite. The sharp little nose, the bow mouth, the dark lashes sweeping over flushed cheeks. She rocks slightly on her knees, and I get a whiff of her upturned cunt.

"Enjoying this?" I ask, and she flushes further. How delightful.

"You're doing so well. Tell me, what made you crawl for me?"

She licks her lips before answering. "I thought...you wanted.."

"I did, pet. I did, and you did it beautifully. But I want to know why you, Selene, why you would choose to crawl for me."

"I lost the bet."

"Did you?"

She turns her head so her hair veils her face. I could order her to look at me, but I'll give her the illusion of privacy. "I guess...I wanted to please you."

Truth. I straighten, triumphant. Her scent confirms her desire.

"Poor, sweet pet. I've neglected you all day. Come." I hold open my arms. Biting her lip, she crawls up onto my lap. I put two fingers against her mouth.

"Did you enjoy your day?"

She nods and I take my fingers away. "Speak."

"Who were the shifters who visited today?

"Did you like them, pet? I thought they would provide much needed entertainment."

"They said they were looking into my pack."

"Yes. I want to find them."

"Why?"

"To corroborate your story, of course." She stiffens in my arms. Aha. "Do you not want me to find them?"

"I...it's been a long time."

"You could return to them, if you wish."

She blinks at me. "What?"

"After this...experience. Once we've had our fun. Did you think I'd keep you forever?" I prod her, enjoying her wide-eyed expression.

"You'd let me go?"

"Why not? You can stay if you wish." I stroke her rigid back. "There will always be a place for you in my club. I'll take care of you. Or if you want to return to your family, you can."

Her head bows and her hair veils her face. "My family is dead."

I make a fist behind her back. I'd forgotten. "My apologies," I say, and mean it. She peeps at me from behind the shimmering fall of her hair. "I meant I will return you to your kind, if you wish it."

She's biting her lip again, looking past my French double doors, worry knotted on her forehead.

"Relax, pet. I only meant to give you a gift."

"A gift," she echoes.

"A kindness. After our time together, I will not keep you caged. Wild animals are meant to run free." I brush the hair back from her tense face. "What are you thinking, pet?"

"I don't know what to think. I never thought you'd set me free."

I set my fingers around her neck, collaring her. "Not yet, pet. First, you earn it."

She licks her lips, visibly reining in her focus. "What do you want me to do?"

"Come," I rise with her in my arms. "I'll show you."

I head to the door with Selene stiff in my arms. She always seems uncertain of what to do when I carry her, and I enjoy putting her off balance.

The guards see me coming and pull open the doors. "Mr. Frangelico," they greet me and usher me to the limo. I set Selene on the floor of the limo and take my seat. She looks a little dazed, so I snap my fingers and point to a place in front of my seat. She scoots closer and settles into a submissive's pose gracefully. I sift my fingers through her hair and pull her head to my knee.

"Relax, pet," I order. She blows out a breath hard enough to stir her hair, but the tension in her shoulders eases.

The limo rolls down the street, heading for my business holdings. I had Tucson on my radar for years before I moved in. My stay in Hollywood left me tired and jaded, even for a two thousand-year-old vampire. The production company I founded still pours money into my coffers, but when the time came to fake my death and move on, I was more than happy to find a new town to haunt. LA, for all it's glamour, feels old. A shrine where virgins sacrifice themselves for fame.

We pass a movie theater plastered with posters of the latest blockbuster. The starring actress came to stardom through my agency. She was one of my finds. She offered to fuck me for a role, but by then I was tired of it all. Tired of the fake tans, the airbrushed photos. The wheeling and dealing and greed that surpasses everything, even desire for human contact. When sex is a tool, a weapon to win a final role, life becomes more hollow than even a jaded vampire can bear. I came to Tucson—retreated is more like it—to find something real. Two bodies, colliding in the night. Untempered, uncalculated passion.

It's no use. People look at me and they see my role. Vampire King. Ancient ruler. Even my sired eventually turn on me, try to take my power. Mine is the first face they see when they rise as vampires, and mine is the last. They attack and I kill them. One by one, the stars go out and I am left alone, in the dark.

"Sir?" A soft voice at my knee. "Are you all right?"

I'm sighing like a Victorian fop. The men of that era were useless, though a few wrote half decent poetry.

"I'm fine, pet. Just a little...stressed."

Selene blinks up at me, dark lashes framing ocean grey eyes. She isn't afraid of me, not really. Her wolf seems to accept me. It surged to the fore during the day, when I couldn't protect her.

Her hair washes over my leg and I finger the silky strands. "Selene," I say out loud, and lift a lock of hair to my lips. She flushes like I've kissed a very personal part of her—which I intend to do. Soon. "Goddess of the moon. Fitting name for a werewolf."

She sniffs. "That's a myth. We don't have to shift with the moon."

"There are many false myths about us. Both our kinds.

For one thing, I enjoy garlic."

She smiles at that. "The garlic stuffed olives tipped me off. You're Italian, right?"

I raise my brow at her direct question.

"Sorry," she looks away.

"No, you're not," I chide, tugging her hair. She's not sorry at all.

"Is it rude to ask questions about a vampire's past?"

"Not rude. Impertinent. You're lucky I enjoy it. But be careful, pet. Push too far, and I'll gag that sweet mouth." Her eyelashes flutter and I sit back. "I spent some centuries in Italy, yes. Turf wars between the city states. Whoring and dining with the Medicis. It grew tiresome, and the church's increased focus on finding and burning out any evil or witches became uncomfortable. I escaped to the New World, with plenty of wilderness and cover for monsters who hunt at night."

"You think you're a monster?" she whispers to the carpet.

"I know I am. A creature of hunger and darkness. The older I get, the more my perversions."

Her throat convulses. "You hurt people."

"I do," I drawl, deepening my voice. "I enjoy it." I tug her head back, exposing her neck. "So do you."

Her head jerks and I tighten my grip.

"You deny it?"

"I don't like pain."

"Not just pain." I run a finger from the jaw to the soft column of her throat, enjoying her struggle to keep from lashing out. "Pain, pleasure depends on the way the body registers it. Two sides of the same coin. When I whip a sub," a tremor goes through her at the word *whip*, "I balance them on a knife's edge. Suspended over two chasms. One way—immense pain. The other—boundless pleasure." I hold out my hand and rock it back and forth as she stares. "They never know which way they'll fall."

"So that's it. You like being in control."

"I don't like it, pet." I wind her hair around my fist until she's caught, throat taut, lips quivering, on a white golden leash. "I live for it."

The limo coasts to a halt. I hold her in place one, two, three long moments before releasing her. "Shall we?"

I help her out of the limo and usher her to the club door. The door's unlocked but no one's inside, as I instructed. Selene clings to my arm as we walk through the murky coat check area and descend the stairs into the gloom.

"What is this place?" she asks, voice hushed.

In answer, I press a hidden panel and flick on the first set of lights. The first part of the room is dedicated to lounging. A backlit bar faces an assortment of low tables and plush armchairs. I wait for Selene's eyes to adjust and illuminate the second half of the dungeon. Spotlights appear around the vast room, shining on the heavy wooden furniture bolted to the floor. St. Andrew's crosses, spanking benches, wooden horses, long tables topped with black leather—a well appointed BDSM dungeon. A dom's paradise. A submissive's hell and heaven all in one.

I flip the final switch and entire wall lights up. Selene gasps at the display of hanging floggers, Shibari rope, whips, paddles and canes.

Her shock is refreshing. Was I ever so innocent? Her

head swivels, her wide eyes lit up, taking everything in. Her nipples are sharp points. Not so innocent. At least some part of her is fascinated.

Excellent.

"Well, pet." I touch her hair to awaken her. "What do you think?"

She blinks. Licks her lips. Says the last thing I'd expect: "Nobody expects the Spanish Inquisition."

CHAPTER 5

Selene

THE VAMPIRE KING moves behind me, a giant, dark shadow in this frightening place. His laughter echoes around me, surrounding me like a warm blanket, entering my veins. The sound makes me light headed, like a glass of whiskey on an empty stomach. I sway a little and he wraps a large arm around my waist.

"Welcome to Toxic, pet."

"This place...is yours?" I've heard of the vampire's night club and the rumors of what it really is: a BDSM dungeon with a dance club as a cover. Some vampires are sadists, and prefer their victims to be submissive masochists. Sweetbloods, they call them. The blood has more flavor when mixed with endorphins, the body's response to pain.

"All you see."

"Everything the light touches," I mutter. A smart mouth is a good way to cover up fear. Lucius laughs again, and keeps chuckling as he moves me forward.

We're halfway to the center of the room, where a heavy throne sits on a raised platform, a spotlight showcasing its medieval splendor, when the silence makes sense.

"There's no one here."

"Of course not," Lucius purrs in my ear. "You are my most prized possession. I do not want to show you off, not quite yet."

I think of the party he's throwing in a month. "But someday?"

"Someday." He moves from me, taking his place on the throne. A king in his kingdom. His natural habitat. "Are you ready to begin your training?"

Am I? I turn in place, taking extra time to examine the wall of implements. The Wall of Pain. In training, I've seen worse, felt worse, but this is different. Private. Sensual. There's only the two of us here. Lucius, rolling up his shirtsleeves to expose deliciously strong forearms. Me, with my nipples tenting my romper top and my pussy pulsing.

I'm not scared of the way Lucius might hurt me. I'm scared I might like it.

Lucius snaps his fingers and I'm over beside him in a flash. Kneeling, head bowed, arms boxed behind my back.

"Playtime's over," he tells me. "When we're here, you'll obey my commands or be punished. No excuses, no exceptions. You will call me *sir* at all times, unless I've ordered you not to speak. Understand? You may speak."

I swallow. "Yes, sir."

"I might wish for you to strip, or crawl. You will obey immediately or suffer the consequences. And, pet, you won't like the consequences. Do you have any questions?"

"What are the consequences?" I ask, adding, "Sir?"

His dark eyes twinkle at me. He's enjoying this...scene, game, whatever it is. "Disobey and find out."

My eyes flick to the Wall of Pain. He leans forward and captures my chin, drawing me back. "Obey me and I'll reward you. You will love the rewards. You had a taste of them last night."

Yep. I'll never forget those orgasms. I want more.

"In one month, I will present you to my kingdom. A king's consort. Everyone will covet you. You'll perform for them, and earn your freedom."

"And this," he reaches to the side table and opens a drawer, draws out a box. A heavy silver collar lies on a black velvet cushion. Lucius picks it up and diamonds wink at me. "A collar fit for a queen. I intend to train you for my use, and mine alone. You will kneel for no one...but me."

Interesting. Xavier's intel said nothing about him being this possessive with a submissive.

I open my mouth and wait for the incline of his head giving me permission to speak. "And after the party...sir?"

"You'll be free to come and go as you please. You're free to go back to your pack, if you wish. The price of your freedom is your ultimate submission, but after that, you can take the collar and go."

I rock back on my heels. He intends to train me, make

me want him. I'm a prop in his show of power. If he can get me to do as he commands …

"And if I want to stay?"

"There will always be a place for you here. At my side."

"As your submissive? Or for you to pass around as you please?"

"Our arrangement has a natural end, but I would continue to take care of you. You would work here. You would only submit to vampires you choose."

I tilt my head as if considering it. He thinks he's going to break down my defenses. I'm going to break down his —and the minute he turns his back, I'll turn on him. Everything is going according to plan.

"All right," I say. "I'm ready."

He sweeps a hand out and indicates the Wall of Pain. "Choose."

I straighten. Stare at him and heave a breath before getting to my feet. The rows of implements blur as I get close. I grab the one closest to me, a strip of leather with an angled tip attached to a long handle. When I return to Lucius, I kneel and offer it to him, head bowed. The choreography of high protocol makes things easier, especially when I'm steeling myself for a long night.

Lucius takes the whip and sets it aside before gathering me close.

"Frightened?"

I dip my head.

"Don't be. I won't harm you." His large hands trespass over my body, kneading my shoulders until I melt, finding my resistance, breaking it down. His touch feels good. I both love and hate how I respond to him.

"I don't know if I can do this," I blurt.

"You don't have to do anything. Just be."

"When we're in a scene, I am aware of everything about you—every movement, every flinch, every quiver. Your role is to be aware of me. I will be your world. My words, your god." His large hands cup my face and tip my head back to meet his eyes. "Give yourself to me, Selene. I won't ever let you fall."

∼

Lucius

MY PET SQUIRMS on my lap, too on edge to sit still. She's both nervous and curious, a refreshing combination. I set her on her knees on the floor and fasten the collar around her neck. "High protocol," I tell her and she nods, instantly bowing her head. Her gasp makes me grasp her chin. "What is it, pet?"

"Do you need me?" She eyes the bulge in my slacks. Afraid? Eager? Her face is a mask a vampire would envy.

"Not right now, pet," I tell her. "You must earn it." Her eyes widen slightly. Nervous. She really is a virgin.

"You need a new safeword, pet. Something unique."

"Shrubbery?" she suggests and I bite back a grin.

"That will work."

I sit in silence for a moment, letting her anticipation build. She fidgets, shifting her ass over one heel, then the other. Her wide eyes blink rapidly, breath shortens. She watches my face and I watch her back.

"Stand and disrobe." I keep the order short. Concise.

She immediately jumps to obey. Her romper falls to the floor in a heap and she stands nude before me, her pretty nipples jutting out, her cunt dewy and ripe for the taking.

My cock throbs painfully against my leg, but I'm a master of control. A vampire in my position has to be. I'm not like a rutting wolf, who gives in to his desire and marks his mate viciously. No, I bide my time. Make her tremble. Teach her obedience. My satisfaction comes in my dominion over her, not in some base release of my manhood.

I slowly rise from my throne, picking up a leash and hooking it to her collar. "Come, pet. I'm eager to mark your pale skin again." I take the dragon's tail with me, and a leather paddle.

She doesn't miss any of it, her dilated eyes taking it all in with a flash of alarm. I lift my chin in the direction of a spanking bench. "Over there. Mount the bench, pet."

I don't miss the shiver that runs down her spine, but she obeys wordlessly, kneeling over the bench.

I buckle her wrists and ankles in and check them for tightness. Her pussy looks too delicious not to touch, so I sweep a finger over the dewy slit, spreading her natural lubricant up to her clit.

She arches her ass to me and I spank it, hard.

She's a wolf, so pain means little. Any marks I leave will heal almost immediately. Some vampires love shifter subs for this reason. Some hate them—they prefer humans who will feel the full brunt of punishment for days.

I never had much of an opinion, but in this moment, I'm glad Selene is a little wolf. I'm too protective of her to want her to experience any lasting discomfort, even for pleasure's sake.

"Ready for your spanking, Selene?"

She doesn't answer, so I slap her ass again.

"Yes, sir." Her words are slightly sullen, but I don't miss the breathless quality to them. She's excited but her pride keeps her from admitting it.

I palm the handle of the leather paddle. It's a lovely instrument, flat and slappy. It makes for a great warm up—a little more harsh than the flogger or my hand, but still light and stingy.

I slap it once across the center of her buttocks and listen to her gasp. The mere sound of it gives me pleasure. I smack her again and pause for the reaction. I begin in earnest, slapping fast and quick, all over her pale globes.

The intensity surprises her, because she gasps and squirms, twisting her wrists against the cuffs. I love the way her ass clenches and quivers. After thirty or so strokes, she gets control of herself. The endorphins are starting to kick in as the blood rushes to her ass, turning it a rosy hue. She slows her breath and goes still, taking the spanks bravely.

So, of course, I stop.

"Getting warm, beautiful?" I squeeze one cheek roughly.

She growls a bit, totally unsubmissive.

I chuckle. "I think this ass needs something to clench around while I spank, don't you?"

She's wise enough not to answer.

I get a tube of lubricant from my toolbox and coat a small, stainless steel butt plug with it. "Open for your plug, pet."

She immediately tightens her anus.

I wait.

After a moment, she blows out a breath, relaxing her ass. I press the bulbous tip to her tight rosette and apply slight pressure. After a beat, the muscles release. I push the plug forward and she gives a mewl of alarm.

"Easy, pet. Breathe. Big exhale."

I wait until she obeys, then continue to press the plug in until it seats. She whimpers, a tremor shaking her inner thighs. Her juices leak from her cunt.

"Good girl." I resume spanking with the paddle, lighter this time, but with the intent of jiggling her flesh and causing the plug to twist and move inside of her.

She moans and pants. Squirms and gasps.

I stop and twist the plug, pulling it out an inch before plunging it back inside her. Her gasp of surprise makes me harder than a rock.

"You're not blooded, but is this ass virginal, too, little wolf? You may speak."

"Yes, sir," she whimpers.

"You like it, though, don't you?"

"No!" she gasps immediately.

I pause, waiting for her to correct her mistake, but she doesn't. I pick up the dragon's tail. "No, *sir,* you mean."

"No, sir," she agrees quickly.

"Too late, love." I flick the handle of the implement and the leather braid snaps down across her buttocks.

She gasps and her shoulders tense.

I wait a full ten seconds before I apply a second stroke, then only two beats before the third. I keep the rhythm unpredictable but slow, driving her into a pain-induced euphoria, each biting lash an invitation to sink deeper. To surrender fully.

She does, and quickly. She certainly has been trained in this regard. It's more the pleasure part that appears foreign to her. Who were the idiots who trained her, anyway?

But why am I surprised? So many masters know only cruelty and greed for power. They lack the subtlety necessary to achieve the true balance of dominance and submission.

I stripe her ass thoroughly, then wait, listening to the sound of her frantic breaths. When they quiet, I reward her with a slow nuzzle of her clit.

She moans. I circle it with my forefinger, rub a little harder.

I pump the buttplug at the same time and her breath returns to pants.

"Beg," I command. A single word. One she likely hates.

Her inner thighs quiver. She's wetter than an ocean, but I'm loathe to let her come yet. Especially if she won't beg.

I walk around to the front of the spanking bench, and unzip my pants.

She lifts her blue-grey eyes to my face, lust and confusion warring.

"Please me, Selene, and I'll let you come."

She moistens her lips with the tip of her tongue.

I free my cock and rub it over her generous lips. She

licks around the head with sloppy, uncoordinated movements. It's harder without the use of hands.

I push into her mouth, fuck it. I know lots of doms will change up the rhythm so a sub can't follow it, so she'll choke and gag and grow fearful. I don't play those games. I want her to enjoy pleasuring me, so I make it easy for her. Slow dips into her mouth, not too deep.

Her training shows now. She hollows her cheeks and sucks hard, her tongue swirling underneath my cock.

A shudder of pleasure runs through me, right down to my heels.

This little wolf...she does such things to me.

I grip the back of her head and fuck her mouth faster. "Good girl. Such a good cock-suck, aren't you? Keep it up...just like that." Pleasure gets on top of me, far before I expect it. My eyes roll back in my head.

"I'm coming," I warn. I spend in her mouth and she swallows my essence down without complaint.

I stroke her hair back, run my thumb over her soft cheek. "Good girl," I praise. "You've pleased your master."

She lifts her gaze to mine, steady. There's an unspoken appeal there.

"Yes, I'll let you come, now, beautiful. You deserve the reward."

I don't unbuckle her. I want her captive for this. I stroke around behind her and fuck her with the plug a few times before I pull it out. Then I lick her from clit to anus and back again. I push her thighs open and feast between her legs, exploring her folds, fucking her with my tongue.

When she's moaning, I stop and spank her pussy—five firm swats.

She shrieks and moans, twists against the leather cuffs holding her ankles and wrists.

I repeat the whole thing—first treating her with my tongue, then pussy-spanking her. Four more rounds and she's a sobbing wreck.

"Please… please, sir. Let me come. I need to come now. Please, I can't take it any more," she babbles.

"You think you deserve to come now?" I spank her pussy.

"Yes! Yes, sir."

I spank her again, three more times. I twist my little finger inside her tight channel and finger fuck her.

"You may come." I manage to sound regal. Imperial, even, but I'm actually as moved as she is, lust rocketing through my limbs despite the fact that I just came in her mouth.

Something about seeing my proud, beautiful wolf so undone excites me more than anything has in the last century.

Be careful, Lucius. Don't let this one get under your skin. Lose focus and you'll miss the direction of the coup.

Selene's walls squeeze my pinkie like a vise and her thighs quake as she comes and comes, her belly heaving against the padded leather bench, her bare breasts rubbing it with each breath.

I stifle a groan.

When she's finished, I unbuckle her, wrap her up in a blanket and carry her to my throne. "You all right, pet?" I settle in my chair, with my treasured cargo in my lap.

Her head falls back, her mouth curved and eyes hazy with bliss. "I'm not dead yet."

I chuckle.

"I will consume you as you consume me, and if we're very lucky pet, we won't both die of pleasure."

It was a mistake, keeping her a virgin. For all her strength, she has no defenses against a slow seduction.

I enjoy her warm weight. She turns in my arms, mumbles something.

"What's that, pet?" I smooth her hair down her back.

"I didn't know it would feel this way," she whispers.

"How does it feel?"

Her lips shape the words but barely any sound comes out. "Good. It feels good."

CHAPTER 6

*S*elene

"It's almost dawn. We need to go," Lucius tells me. I jerk awake his arms.

"I lost track of time." This night has lasted a moment and forever. If I didn't know any better, I'd think Lucius enjoyed cuddling me on his throne. He doesn't let me walk to the car, either, settling into the seat.

The shadows play over his patrician features as the car moves. Even if he wasn't the King of the Vampires, Lucius would be quite a catch.

His looks are part of his power, the fine blade of beauty able to cut deep. Being the sole focus of all that beauty and power is a heady experience. Is this what he does every night? Tie up submissives and dazzle them?

When I ask him, his lips curve—either because of my question, or because of my cheek. "Not every night. And I don't need to tie anyone up. I'm dominant to everyone I meet."

"I know that." I almost roll my eyes, stopping myself from being a brat. "I meant—"

"I know what you meant, pet," he interrupts, and continues gently, "I've never reserved the club for my personal use before."

"Oh," I try to ignore the warmth curling through me. I can't help it. I feel special. Lucius looks amused and I mentally kick myself. I shouldn't care what Lucius thinks of me. I shouldn't be like this, relaxed and happy in his arms.

I try to escape and his hold tightens. His lips find my ear. "Do I dazzle you?" He nuzzles my hair.

"No," I lie. His arms squeeze me as he laughs. Gah, that laugh. I could live in it.

"I think I do."

I bite my lip, wishing I was better at hiding from him.

"Will you tell me about her? Your vampire lover?"

Lucius sighs. He leans back in the seat, taking me with him. For a few minutes he's silent, nuzzling my hair like he's a big dog fascinated by a kitten. I should be stiff and scared, trapped in the arms of a bigger predator, but no, my silly wolf likes the attention. "Georgianna was my first submissive. My last. There have been other submissives I've employed at the club, ones I've shared with other vampires, but none like her. I met her when she was still human, but even as a vampire, she was so alive. So full of life."

"Did you turn her?"

"No. She belonged to another." His lip curls. "He took advantage of her sweet nature and turned her."

My throat's clogged up. Why did I even ask? He obviously loved Georgianna. Maybe her death made him the ruthless ruler he is today. "You didn't approve?"

"I'm no hypocrite. I wanted her as much as he did, but I would've done things differently. Creating a vampire...requires a delicate balance of power. They're so dependent in the beginning. Physically as well as emotionally." He stares out the window at the passing desert. "In the beginning, they will do anything to please you."

"And later?"

I sense the change before his fingers retreat. I want to push into his hand, beg silently for the return of his touch like an eager pet.

"Eventually they hate you." His tone is formal, distant. "All that love runs out."

When the limo stops, the sky over the mountains is lighter, the night easing to make way for the dawn. We're cutting things close, but Lucius doesn't seem to mind.

He insists on carrying me into his home and bathing me. His cock is so hard it juts out from his body, but he makes no move to satisfy himself again. Lucius the ruler makes way for Lucius the good dom, taking consummate care of his charge without a hint of cruelty or selfishness. He washes and dries me, carrying me to my room. He lays me on the bed and spreads my hair out on a towel so the wet strands won't touch my pillow, and the whole time his doting mask never slips.

I have to remember that he's a monster. A murder of

innocents. I can't forget what he did to my family, my pack.

But when I search his face, I find no hint of cruelty in the patrician lines of his face. He runs his fingertips lightly over my neck and forehead, and I drift deeper under his spell. My mind holds fast to my plan for revenge, but my body is all too willing to forget.

"How many vampires have you turned?" I ask as he stretches out beside me on his side, propping his head up on his left hand, leaving his right hand free to play with my hair.

"Too many too count."

"Are they all here? In Tucson?"

"Yes. They follow me. In the beginning they are dependant on my blood to survive. I wean them, but old habits die hard."

"Wow. I didn't know there were that many vampires here." Tucson's big, but not that big. If he's turned countless vampires and they're all here... How many square miles does each vampire need to hunt? Do they divide territory by distance or population and potential victims? Either way, it's a wonder the human news hasn't gotten wind of them. Strange disappearances, blooded corpses...

"You misunderstand, pet. There aren't that many of my sired left."

"Why not?"

I told you, pet, they turn on me. I don't allow insubordination. Traitors don't live long."

"Oh," I say weakly. "Of course not."

Lucius keeps playing with my hair like we're talking about the weather. He takes a strand and brushes it against my cheek, murmuring, "How do you think my maker died?"

I can't believe I'm lying here, next to the Vampire King, talking death and politics. "I guess you didn't become king by mandate of the masses," I mumble.

He chuckles, and keeps tickling my face with my hair.

"What happened to Georgianna? Is she still alive?"

"No," Lucius says, and pulls his hand away. I press my lips together, keeping my questions in, and after a few moments he resumes stroking my brow.

I stare at the ceiling. Outside, the sky lightens to a rich navy blue. The high windows frame one bright star. Venus. The morningstar. Dawn's coming, and any second Lucius will leave me.

For now, he seems content to lie beside me and watch me. Is this normal? Am I so fascinating? Two thousand years, and his maker and his lover both died at his hands, along with countless vampires he sired.

"So, over the years, one way or another, everyone close to you has died?"

The heavy silence is my answer.

"Sounds lonely," I tell the ceiling.

"Pet," his sigh creaks in my ear. "you have no idea."

Selene

OVER THE NEXT FEW DAYS, I fall into a dream. Lucius must

have shut down Club Toxic for the whole week, because he takes me there again and again to train me.

"I'm going to break you in, pet. Bring you to heel…"

Maybe it's what he told me of Georgianna, or how much I look like her, but I find myself striving for Lucius' approval as if I'm competing with his first submissive.

I'm not jealous of his first love. I'm not. I just want to entice Lucius as he entices me.

I tell myself I'm being smart, gathering intelligence. But I haven't made any inroads to finding a way to get his guard down. The only time he lets his guard down is after a scene, and I can't exactly stake him during aftercare. He wouldn't expect it, but I'm in no position to outmaneuver him, not while I'm recovering from the ecstasy he unleashes.

There are stretches when Lucius leaves me to run his empire, but he works me over beforehand. I sleep while he's gone, and when I wake, he's with me, ready to play again.

One night, after a heady session, I wake to him leaning over me.

"What—?" I croak and he shushes me.

"It's all right, my pet. It's just a nightmare." The question must show on my face because he explains. "You were crying out in your sleep."

"I…" I swallow to wet my throat. "I was?"

"Here." He hands me a glass of water. I often wake to find water and chocolate on my bedside table. His way of caring for me if he can't be here when I wake.

I drink and rub my face, clearing the cobwebs out of the corners of my mind. I've had nightmares since my family was killed, but no one, not even my foster mother, ever entered my room to comfort me. I've always been alone.

The bed dips and he surrounds me, his large body curling around mine. He's so big, I'm swallowed up in his embrace. My feet only reach his calves. I crane my head to look back at him. "What are you doing?"

"Can't I spend the night with my sub?" He brushes the hair off my bare shoulder and kisses my neck. His left arm snakes around my middle, gathering me against him when I would tighten into a ball. This is nuts.

The Vampire King wants to cuddle? What planet am I on?

"Time to sleep." he whispers. "No more monsters under your bed. I'm the only monster here." There's a self mocking twist to his voice. "And you don't have to be afraid of me. Not tonight."

I close my eyes, willing myself to ignore his presence. It doesn't work. Head to toe, his body touches me, and even if he leaves my bed later, he'll be the first thing on my mind when I rise. The last thing I think of when I fall asleep.

I'm forgetting to hate him.

CHAPTER 7

Selene

THE NEXT DAY, I'm running as a wolf, sniffing at an old rabbit trail, when something flutters above my head. A piece of paper blowing in the breeze. I catch the paper under my paw. My body goes solid. A copy of an old photograph. Even faded, the lines of the image are clear. I crouch behind the cactus, my wolf whimpering. I can't stop myself from pushing the paper flat and looking closer, even though I know what the photo shows. I've seen it a thousand times. Xavier hung it on the wall of the gym where I learned to spar. I'd fight hooded opponents until my muscles screamed, and when I fell—eventually I always fell—I'd look up at the picture, grit my teeth. I'd endure a beating night after night, staring at the photo of the massacre. I'd limp to the showers, wash the blood off my skin, and fall into bed, stifling a groan. I'd lie there, body one giant bruise, the photograph etched in my mind's eye.

Bodies lie in a room, sprawled where they fell. I remember the room—an old Elk lodge converted into a community center. The pack hangout, with an old pool table and a faded Ansel Adams poster curling on the wall. Here's one wolf curled around his mate, protecting her even in death. Here's another facing the camera, eyes dulled, throat torn out.

This is what Lucius did to my pack. I don't know why he sentenced them to death. Xavier told me only a few were bitten. The younger ones, the ones who put up the most fight, Lucius took from the lodge and held in his private lair, drinking from them until they died. Xavier doesn't have photos of that, only reports from eye witnesses.

The breeze tugs at the paper, and I plant a paw in the middle. Xavier left this here for me. He and his people are watching me right now. He knows I've been weak. He knows I need a reminder. He doesn't want me to forget why Lucius has to die.

Old pain cracks my heart, poisons my blood.

I nudge a rock onto the photo to hold it down while I dig a hole. Gotta bury the evidence that Xavier was here.

Once the photo is buried in a hole by the cactus, I return to my room, shift and change into a tight camisole and loose pair of shorts. Somewhere in this house is the clue to Lucius' lair. Vampires are smart, secretive, viper-fast. Ultimate predators. But during the day they sleep like the dead. I've already infiltrated his house, and played the role of submissive until I'm left free and unsupervised during the day. If I can find his sleeping place, I could stake him. My mission could be over by sundown.

I exit my room and start searching. I'm looking for cameras, hidden panels, anything that might clue me into a secret entrance to a safe room, or an underground chamber. I wander through the well-appointed rooms, noting a fancy wooden chair. I grab it and snap off its leg, and use a kitchen knife to sharpen a stake.

As I walk down the hall, cameras track my movements. After a few minutes my search is going to be obvious. Lucius will know what I'm up to. The wolf's out of the bag, and I will have to explain my actions to an already paranoid king. If I don't find and kill him, tonight my life will be forfeit.

I better find his lair.

All afternoon I search as the sun sinks, a natural countdown clock. By the time the house is filled with thick, golden light of oncoming dusk, I've forgotten all semblance of discretion. I tear through bedrooms, ripping at wall hangings and paintings, running my fingers over every lintel, chair rail, and piece of crown moulding. I rap on walls and pull books off shelves, feeling for false panels.

"Come on, come on," I breathe, feeling behind a piece of shelving with one eye on the window. My wolf is frantic, clawing to the surface, fighting to protect me. I'm in a race with the dying sun, and I'm losing.

Vampires as old as Lucius have more than the usual defenses, Xavier once told me.

Lucius is old, but he's embraced modern times. He'll have extra layers of protection, technology and otherwise.

But maybe I've relied too much on finding the signs of tech security.

Stepping to the center of the room, I close my eyes and extend my senses. My wolf is right there, waiting to show me the way. I drop to all fours and sniff around the corners of the room until I come to the unused fireplace. I've sniffed around here in wolf form before, but something nudged me away. A vampire's natural defenses, older than technology, communicating to the primal part of me. *Go away*, the scent around the fireplace says. *Danger here.* Danger, or a vampire?

I crawl into the fireplace, ignoring the creepy crawly sensation running over my skin, and feel around for a lever, a false brick, anything. I don't know what I touch but one minute I'm standing on the painted brick—too pristine to ever have hosted a fire—and the next I'm sliding down a slick tunnel, mouth open in a silent scream. I land on my feet and bound upright, groping blindly in the dark passage. Above my head, light from the bedroom winks at me. I've found the secret passageway to Lucius' lair. Yes!

The panel above snaps shut, sealing me in the dark.

Shit.

I jump and wedge myself in the tunnel so I can bang on it. It doesn't budge. I dig my fingers around the seal, looking for cracks. Nothing.

I drop to my feet and explore the lightless tunnel. It's tight and narrow. Could it even fit Lucius' massive frame? I extend my arms and legs and measure it. It'd be tight, but the Vampire King could fit. At least, I hope so. Otherwise, I've found a false passage. A trap.

As minutes tick by, the walls seem to close in. The air is stale and stifling. I've got a bad feeling about this. How long has it been? Surely it's after dusk. Lucius must be awake. He'll see the destruction I've wreaked on his house, and know what's up. If he finds me I'm dead.

I drop to the floor, curling around my legs. Maybe he won't come for me. If he knows I'm a spy, he could leave me here, in this dark, airless prison. A little wait, and I wouldn't be his problem any more. It would only take three days...

Light cracks above my head and I heave in relief. Fresh air flows over my face. I launch myself up and scrabble through the tight space, desperate for the light. I emerge from the tunnel, half hyperventilating, half crying, and heave myself over the fireplace threshold. Sweet freedom.

Someone clears their throat above me. Lucius' bare feet stand a few feet away. I push to my feet and lunge.

The stake slices through the air. Lucius blurs away. Fucker's so fast. I flail off balance. A big hand hooks around my leg and makes me crash to the floor. A kick to my wrist and I drop my weapon. He kicks the stake away. It rolls into the fireplace and disappears in the trap with a clatter.

I flop on the carpet like a caught fish and squint against the bright light. Not daylight, not anymore. The sun is down. My time's run out.

Lucius' leans over me. . "You've been a busy little pet," he murmurs without amusement. "Sticking your cute nose where it doesn't belong. How shall I punish you?" The coldness in his tone makes me shiver.

I pant on the carpet. I played my card, and he knows I'm his enemy.

I am so fucked.

Lucius

My sweet pet quivers on the floor. The past few nights, I've been in this position often, looming over her while she lolls in ecstasy at my feet. BDSM is a game where everyone wins.

Tonight, it's no game. I knew she was here for something, but I didn't think she'd be so brazen as to believe she could best me.

Now I know. The gloves have come off.

"I'm flattered, pet. You've gone through so much trouble to find me." I sweep a mocking glance over the room's destruction.

She flops onto her back and glares up at me. A fighter to the last. "Get this over with."

"What do you think I'm going to do?"

She shrugs and rolls away, coming into a crouch. Even standing, she'd be no match for me, and she knows it. "I don't know. Kill and torture me?"

"So you do expect the Spanish Inquisition." I smirk as I reference her Monty Python joke.

She doesn't smile.

"Maybe I will torture you. Find out the real reason you're here, but a vampire against a shifter is hardly sporting odds." I tilt my head to the side. "Who put you up to this?"

"No one," she snarls.

"No?" As smart as Selene is, the auction, getting me to bid on a woman who looks like my lost Georgianna—the whole plan stinks of vampire. My sired have to be behind this, along with Xavier. "So you want to kill me? Why?"

"Revenge."

That makes me pause. "Revenge?"

"For the ones you killed."

"Ah, pet. You'll have to be more specific," I mock. "I'm very old, and I've had many victims. Are these humans I've killed? Did I first suck their blood?"

"Fuck you," she snaps, rolling to her feet. Her gaze darts longingly to fireplace. She's wishing for the stake.

"Perhaps later. Right now, I'm in the mood for a game." I step back and unbutton my shirt.

She's frozen, ready to flee. "What are you doing?"

"Getting ready for the game." I drop my shirt.

"What game?"

"Have you heard of take-down play? No? No matter, pet. It's very simple. You run, and I catch you, and when I catch you, I win. Are you ready?"

Her head twitches back and forth. Wide-eyed, she backs away.

"Too bad. It's time," I tell her, and when she pauses, I hiss, "Run."

Face blank, she darts to the door. I give her a head start, waiting until she hits the door to stalk behind her. Her pale legs flash down the hall and skid into the living room. I put on a burst of vampire speed and watch her race through the house. By the time she reaches the french double doors she's almost on all fours. A white wolf sails across the patio and bounds into the desert. A pale flash of fur, she's heading towards the mountain range. I follow, alternately walking and blurring with supernatural speed. She runs and runs, but never increases the distance between us.

I can tell the moment she realizes she can't outrun me. She slows her bounds and points her muzzle my way, her common sense taking over.

I flash ahead of her. Shifters are fast, but vampires faster. I run so fast I blur, but she's expecting it. At the last second she dodges out of the way, ducking under a cactus. I miss her, but an aggrieved yelp tells me she's learned hiding under a spiny plant isn't the smartest move.

I stalk around the saguaro and find her whimpering on the ground, spines in her side where she brushed too close to a barrel cactus.

Seeing her hurt, my anger drops away.

"Poor pet," I croon. She struggles when I crouch beside her, but after I snap my fingers, she holds still. I pull the long cactus needles out of her. I search through her thick pelt to find each one while she lies docile as a golden retriever.

"Shift," I order and she does, back to human form. Her skin is already healing. She moves into a crouch and yelps, arching off the ground.

"Oops," I lean down and remove the needle from her hip. "Missed one. Are you hurt?"

"Just a flesh wound," she mutters.

Even when I'm angry with her, she makes me laugh. I run a hand down her flank, checking for more spines.

"Stop." She scoots out of reach.

"Excuse me?" My voice is dangerously soft.

"Just stop." Her head is bowed. She knows she's been naughty. "Stop being so nice to me."

Ah. My actions confuse her. Good.

"You disappointed me, pet." I wipe my hands clean. "And you're going to pay."

Her eyes flash. She's not cowed, not by a long shot. "What will you do to me?"

I cup her chin. "Don't worry, pet. I'm not going to kill you. You're too much fun."

Her face twists and she tries to jerk her head away. I cup both hands around her head and she snaps, "Do your worst."

"Oh I will," I promise. "But I don't want to hurt you beyond what you can take. You know why?"

"Because you're a sick fuck," she mutters, her eyes sliding away.

"Perhaps. But you, Selene, you intrigue me. You don't want to submit, yet you do."

"That's not true. It's an act."

"It's not. It's who you are."

"You don't know me. You don't know who I am. What I am."

"All the more reason to keep you alive. You'll tell me your secrets, one by one."

"You could mind wipe me. Make me love you. Then it would be over."

"I told you I'd never mind wipe you. I keep my promises, pet."

She closes her eyes. She looks as tired as I feel. Someone must have put her up to this plan, and that someone should pay. "You're so young. Too young to be so jaded. Innocent…"

"I'll never love you," she blurts.

My eyes widen. "Love, pet? I never said anything about love. I've lived two thousand years on this earth, most as a creature of darkness. Everyone I've ever loved has died. Love is nothing. Fleeting. Emotion. In the end, everything crumbles to dust. Everything."

"Except you," she says, struggling upright. "You live on and on and on."

I should correct her cheekiness, but she's right.

"You should let me kill you. It'd be a mercy."

She so sincere, I burst out laughing. "You are refreshing, pet. The first to convince me to end my life because of my…what's the word…Ennui?"

"You're not happy." she insists. "You are sick of living. Anyone can see it. After a while, what is the point?"

"Living. Living is the point."

"A life without love," she says. "Is it worth it?"

"No. No it's not. But love is nothing. A color in the sky before the dawn. Beautiful, fleeting. Dissipates as quickly as it comes."

"Like humans. Like us shifters." Her eyes are closed again, pain creasing her face. She's so young, to be so aware of death. To be fearless in the face of it.

"What's it like? To have a cause?"

She opens her eyes. "Lonely. In some ways I'm as lonely as you."

"Such honesty." I shake my head in awe.

"Well, I thought I was about to die." Her gaze slides to me as if she's still waiting for me to strike the killing blow.

Instead I take a firm hold on her hair, drawing her head back. "All creatures are close to death. You're mortal. Death is only a matter of time. Now, tell me. Why are you trying to kill me? Who put you up to it?"

She presses her lips together.

"I'll get it out of you," I tell her silkily. "One way or another."

"You could just compel me," she looks me straight in the eye. So daring.

"I told you I wouldn't compel you. I keep my promises." Lest she think I am all altruism, I add, "Besides, if I compel you, our game is over. Where's the fun in that?" I tug on her hair, using it like a leash and marching her forward.

She's silent all the way back to the house. Docile as a lamb. Most animals accept their fate when a larger predator catches them. Selene isn't one to accept, I suspect she's more curious about what I'm going to do.

I chain her to a column on the patio while I go inside to make preparations. It's not until I have her lying on her back, tied to a table I've set up inside, that she becomes chatty again.

"Why did you make so many vampires if they're only going to turn against you?

"Because, pet, as you are so fond of reminding me, I

am alone. Despite the truth of what love is, I hold out hope that I will one day have a family who loves me."

"That's sad." She drops her eyes, perhaps realizing I wouldn't be so honest with someone who had longer to live. "Are you hurt by what I've done?"

"What?" I inhale, fighting the urge to laugh again. "No, pet. I knew from the first that you were sent to betray me."

"Since the auction?" she seems horrified.

"Of course."

"Then why did you bid?"

"Seemed like it would be fun."

"So that's all I am? A bit of entertainment?"

"Yes." I cock my head, remember what she blurted earlier. *I'll never love you.* "Why? Did you think you could be more?"

"No," she mumbles and relaxes. She's limp and compliant as I hook up the TENS unit, checking the electricity flow against my own skin. If she thinks tonight will be fun and games, she's in for a big surprise.

When I step back, the corners of her mouth turn up.

"Why are you smiling?"

"Because." Her shoulders sink down as she sighs. "I've done what I came to do."

"Kill me?"

"Or die trying."

"You're not dead yet," I point out.

"I expect you'll take care of that, soon."

"Oh no, pet." I raise the TENS unit with dangling lead wires and shake it in front of her wide eyes. "I'm not going to make it so easy for you."

CHAPTER 8

Selene

I LIE BACK and try to relax as Lucius places patches on my arms. It's just torture. I expected this.

"Let's start with something easy," he murmurs and holds the square box right where I can see each button. He twists the dial and electricity zaps the skin under the patch. *Breathe, just breathe.* If I relax, the sensation doesn't hurt as much, even when he thumbs the dial further and makes my arm jump.

He places more patches on my hips and tops of my legs. The restraints keep me from closing my legs, but he ignores the thin, sensitive spots on my inner thighs...for now. The current goes from nothing to the highest voltage, making me jolt My muscles contract, spasm, and finally relax, overwhelmed by the current. He's avoiding any tender places that got pierced with cactus spines, and stimulating my large muscles. It doesn't hurt—it actually feels good, like a massage.

A few minutes of getting used to electricity buzzing over my skin and he moves the electrodes, covering my nipples with patches.

"This should be interesting." The first surge shoots straight between my legs and detonates there.

"Fuck me," I throw my head back, gritting my teeth.

"No, pet. Not until you earn it." Lucius isn't playing. He moves the electrodes closer to my labia. My pussy is plump and aching. Each pulse of electricity makes my inner muscles spasm.

"So wet," Lucius tsks. "I wonder…" The buzzing comes in short bursts, tingling in my sensitive bits, driving my arousal higher. By the time he turns the unit off, I'm whimpering, my hips working helplessly. I don't know if I want him to stop or give me more…

"Look at you," he murmurs, running a finger through the sopping mess between my legs. "You love this." He toys with my clit, watching my face closely.

"Stop…" I whisper.

"Why, pet? Because it hurts? Or because you like it?"

I bite my lip so I don't answer, *Both*. His dark chuckle raises hairs on my arms. He holds the unit in front of my face so I can watch him turn the dial all way up. The current buzzes along my lower lips, making them plump. My body reads the electric current as painfully pleasurable, responding to the stimulation. My clit is a lightning rod. Another minute, and my climax sears through me, my brain blanking with white heat.

He moves one of the patches between my ass cheeks,

covering my sensitive back hole. I clench down, my face burning as my orgasm rises. "No…"

"You like it?" he asks.

In vain, I press my lips together. Another round ending in an orgasm, and I'm moaning.

"Let's try something different." He picks up a violet wand tipped with a glass tube and takes his time shocking me. My breasts swell.

Is he torturing me? Or taking me to a new height of pleasure? I spiral higher and higher, but the higher I go, the further I'll fall.

"Why are you here?" he murmurs, taking a break from zapping me. "Who put you up to it? Why do you want to kill me?"

"You killed my pack," I burst out.

"Your pack," he repeats, brow furrowed.

Is he for real? I strain in my bonds. I've never wanted to behead a vampire so badly. "You don't remember? I know you're a monster, but forgetting an entire massacre—"

"Be silent." He paces at the foot of the table, pausing to drum his fingers between my bound feet. "You say I killed your entire pack? How did they die?"

"Slaughtered in their territory. In their clubhouse, in their homes." My family, too, but I don't mention them.

"I've never killed an entire pack. One werewolf, perhaps. Or several, in a fight, but only because they were in a vampire's thrall and attacked first."

I grit my teeth, yanking on the cuffs. Tears burn my eyes, but I refuse to let them fall, to show weakness in front of this monster. Somehow it's worse that he won't acknowledge what he's done. "You killed them."

"Who told this?"

I shake my head.

"Did they have proof?"

"Yes."

"Proof that it was me, and not another? Another vampire?" He rounds the table, coming to stand by my head.

I glare at him. "It was you." It had to be. What reason would Xavier have to lie?

"Think about it," he advises softly. His fingers drift across my chest, stroking the valley between my breasts. I should rant and rail, throw off his touch, but my back arches, pushing my breasts up, begging for the pleasure he can give me. "I don't kill innocents."

"You're lying." I fight against the delicious sensation.

"I have no reason to," he continues, perfectly reasonable. "Why would I take out an entire pack and cover it up?"

"I don't know. You're a sick fuck."

He tuts. "So feisty for someone hooked up to a TENS unit. Tell you what, pet. Please me tonight, and I'll give you Declan's number, and a phone to call him. You can see what he's dug up."

I shake my head. "I don't know what game you're playing, but it won't work."

"I'm not playing a game. I'm playing with you.'

For the next few minutes, he toys with me, wringing climax after climax from my resistant body. He kneels beside the table, keeping his face close to me, as my naked body writhes above him.

It's not until he gives me a break, shutting off the electric current and removing all electrodes before giving me a drink of water, that I tell him,

"Declan won't find anything about my pack. They're all dead. Someone killed them."

HE OFFERS me another sip of water, holding the bottle for me and wiping spilled drops from my lips. "He and his friends are very good at digging up the truth. At least, they're always poking their noses into messes. You can speak to them later."

"If I survive tonight," I pant.

"Yes." His dark eyes glint, but he's not trying to kill me. Not like Xavier said he would.

If I'd attacked Xavier like I attacked Lucius, I'd be dead.

"Had enough water?" Lucius asks. I nod, and turn my head to hide a smile. Even when 'torturing' me, he's keeping my hydrated.

"Why are you smiling?"

"Nothing. You're such a good dom."

"Yes," he leans close, "I never break my toys. Not when they're so much fun. Now, tell me," the mischievous light falls away and we're back in scene. "How did you come to be in the auction?"

I close my eyes. I can't betray my mentor.

"I'll get it out of you," Lucius vows. He doesn't, but he does his best.

"Do you hate me?" I pant when he takes another break. This time he releases my arms and legs and gives them a good rub down before tying me back down.

"No, pet. I don't hate you."

"Then what? What will you do with me?"

He raises the violet wand, running a finger over the crackling bulb. With the lights down low and his face lit by the wand's eerie glow, he looks like a mad scientist. "I told you from the first. I'm going to make you mine."

~

Lucius

"No, no, no," she mewls. My pet is so strong, but after hours of endless orgasms, even the strongest sub will break.

"Take it, pet." I twist the dildo in her and turn up the TENS unit it's attached to, stimulating her deeply.

"No," She drops her head, tears running down her face. "I can't."

"You're not dead yet," I repeat the Monty Python joke, and wring another climax from her unwilling body.

"Has anyone died from too many orgasms?" she mumbles. I brush back her hair and make her drink a glass of water before giving her a cruel smile.

"Let's find out."

The sky outside is lightening. Dawn's an hour away and I need to be safely locked in my crypt well before. I towel her off and release her from the table, coming to her side to help her wobble to the props I've set up in front of the open patio doors.

She leans in to me, her face soft and shining. So submissive. Her obedience lurks under her hard exterior, waiting for a dom strong enough to unlock her true self. That dom is me.

She doesn't fight me as I set her on a leather unit and secure her wrists and ankles. "These bonds will automatically unlock at a certain time."

"What is this?" She blinks at the smooth half circle between her legs.

"A Sybian."

Her eyes widen as she recognizes the brand name. She's basically sitting on a giant vibrator, and she knows it.

"Now," I squat in front of her. "I'll play a little game with you. You're going to sit here and—" I stop as she tosses her head back and forth.

"I can't—"

"Hmm," I pretend to think. "Then, how about this. Tell me who you're working for. Tell me and I'll go after them. You can lie down, take a little nap…"

"You're torturing me with orgasms?"

I smirk. "Didn't expect that, did you?"

"Yes, well. Nobody expects orgasm torture."

I duck my head to hide my smile, and take the moment to check her bonds, making her wiggle her fingers and toes, testing her circulation.

"Lucius," she whines as I rise. "I can't do this."

"I know, pet, I know. It's so hard." I mock her. I'm going easy on her and she knows it. Everything between us is a game. "But it's what you signed up for, isn't it? Night after night, at my mercy."

"I feel like Sheherazade," she mumbles. "Instead of a story, I have to come for you."

"Does that make me a mad sultan?" I stroke my chin and laugh at the look she gives me. Selene makes me laugh more in a day than I have in a century.

"You're mean."

"How should I behave, when I find you were plotting to murder me? Did you think you could waltz in and find my hidden lair? Did you think it would be so easy?"

She bites her lip and I continue, "Don't feel bad. I knew you were plotting against me."

"You did?"

"Of course. It was all so obvious—your resemblance to Georgianna, the auction. What else could you be but a plant?"

"If you knew then why…?"

"Why what, pet?"

"Why did you go through all this trouble?" She jerks her hands in her bonds. "To bring me here. To train me. To make me fall—"

"Make you what?"

"Make me come. Do all these intense things but make me enjoy it. Make me feel good."

"Have I done that? I suppose I couldn't resist mastering you in this way. You fight so deliciously, and in the end—"

"I lose?"

"Oh no, pet. You win. We both do." I raise the Sybian

remote and flick the on switch. The unit comes alive with a subtle buzz.

"No, Lucius," Selene writhes on the leather seat, panting. "I can't."

"Tell me who you're working for. Who sponsored you in the auction and planned all this."

She shakes her head and I increase the force of the vibrations. Her head jerks back and she cries out, her chest flushing with climax after climax. I leave her for a few minutes and return with two more toys.

"Oh thank you," she sobs when I release her, letting her off long enough to drink some water and have some food. She struggles when I lead her back to the unit, whimpering when she sees the two dildos I've affixed to the top. Double penetration will provide far more than double the torture.

"Now, now, pet. This isn't supposed to be fun."

"You're evil," she gasps, sinking down. Her face goes tense as the dildos disappear in her pussy and ass.

"You're good," I murmur. "So very, very good. Now,"—I crouch in front of her—"We're going to play a little game. I'm going to retire for the day and leave you like this—" She whimpers and I raise my voice. "Because I want you to experience something I can't."

"What's that?" Her voice is sharp, frightened. She thinks I'm going to leave her on the Sybian all night.

I won't. I'm not that cruel. I have a timer set so the machine will turn off and the bonds will release in an hour.

"I want you to watch the sunrise."

She goes still, eyes wide.

"That's what I'd do, if I was alive. I'd never miss another dawn."

She's tense, trembling, her body wracked with anticipation of the coming climaxes. I comb her hair back with my fingers and knead her tight neck. Her pulse thuds under my palm.

"Enjoy it, pet. Your life is short, but at least you have the light." And I leave her to witness what I no longer can.

Selene

I TUG and tug but it's no use. The bonds hold fast. I could gnaw off my own arm, of course. If I was in a more gruesome situation, I would. But something tells me Lucius isn't lying when he says he won't kill me...yet. This is a game to him. He takes too much enjoyment out of causing me pain. Why would he leave me strapped to a Sybian after forcing me to orgasm over and over again?

It's been about a half an hour since he left. My internal muscles ache from clenching. My clit is raw from me rocking my hips down on the goddamn dildo. Between my legs, the machine hums along. It's on a setting where the vibrations increase and decrease in waves. I get a few seconds of relief before my orgasm builds again towards another painful peak.

Watch the sunrise. Of all the ridiculous things. Lucius is crazy. Old age drives these vampires to madness.

I lean forward, wishing I could lift off the dildos.

Having them vibrate inside me only reminds me that Lucius hasn't fucked me. Not yet. What the hell is he waiting for?

Past the patio, the desert sprawls in a mess of moonlit creosote and cacti.

A jackrabbit hops across the patio and hesitates, ears outstretched and quivering.

"Move along," I order. That's all I need, the killer rabbit of Caerbannog witnessing my humiliating state. "I mean it. Don't make me come down th-there—" I stutter as the Sybian comes to life. This time vibrations increase rapidly and I moan. My legs clench, my sore pussy convulsing. My labia are numb. If I make it to dawn, I'll be lucky if I can walk.

When I look back up again, the rabbit is gone, disappeared into the desert. The mountain peaks are limned in soft blue, glowing with the approaching light.

Watch the sunrise.

Does Lucius miss it so much? How would I feel if I could never see another sunrise? Never witness sunset? The beauty of the light. I watch as day breaks, pretending it's the last time I'll see one. Memorizing it.

The first touch of sunlight is soft on the mountain face. The birds sing. A few flutter from their perches, safe from predators in the morning light. The earth warms, the red desert coming to life. The shadows shrink into pools of rich darkness stretching from the saguaros. In the heat of the day, those shadows will be welcome, cool places to rest, but right now the darkness flees, the night shrinking, the dawn washing the world clean with light and birdsong. This miracle happens every day, but is anything but mundane. Being forced to witness it almost makes me grateful to the damn vampire.

Almost. As the sun crests the mountain peaks, I gasp through another climax.

Suddenly the Sybian goes silent.

The birds keep chirping. My friend the hare hops between two barrel cactus, sniffing at their fruit.

Behind me the house is empty, its master safely locked in his lair. Lucius has never seen the Tucson dawn, this glorious spectacle. Two thousand years of endless night. A lonely existence in the dark.

The locks on my cuffs click open. I'm free.

Thank fates. Lucius is a merciful king.

At least to me.

I move off the Sybian, the scream of my muscles fading in comparison to the weight in my heart.

And that's when I know.

I don't hate Lucius Frangelico.

~

My muscles scream as I take a quick shower. It'd be nice to fill the bath and soak, but I'm wasting time as it is.

I've got to get out of here. Lucius knows I'm here to kill him. He says he won't kill me, but who knows what kind of games he plays.

Everything's twisted, jumbled. My enemy isn't who he thought he'd be. Or have I lost all perspective?

I dress in jeans and a t-shirt and grab a bag to pack some things when I see it. On the nightstand that was empty before: a cell phone. It's black and basic looking, not a fancy smartphone, but I bet it's untraceable. Lucius fulfilling his promise. *I keep my promises, pet.*

There's one number saved. Declan's.

I press the cell against my mouth. To call or not to call? I could leave, run to Xavier, tell him I failed. I can't kill Lucius.

I mean...I won't.

Even if I could, which I'm not sure is possible, I couldn't bring myself to.

Xavier will destroy me for my failure.

I could run far away, and hope my path never crosses a vampire's again.

Or… I could stay.

Stay with the Vampire King, the supposedly cruel, definitely dominant ruler who's shown me more care and kindness than I've had in years.

My body craves him. Even after what he's done to me. Especially after what he's done to me.

I hit "Call" and put the phone down before I can change my mind. What's the point of calling Declan? Why would I have him investigate my pack? If he somehow figures out it wasn't Lucius...what will I do?

Stupid. I should hang up. I grab the phone just as Declan picks up.

"Hello?" the Irishman's voice is tense.

"It's Selene."

"Jay-sus, I thought ya were Frangelico, calling me in the day. Nearly stopped me heart."

I can't stop my smile. "No, it's just me. I'm Lucius'..." Sub? Lover? Pet? Slave? I make a face.

"I know who ya are, lass," Declan saves me.

"Frangelico called me earlier, said he was turnin' the investigation over tae ya. I can tell ya what we got so far, if ya like."

"I—" The camera in the corner catches my eye. "Yes. Um, first I need to do something. Can I call you back in ten minutes?"

Ten minutes later, I sneak out of the mansion. The desert doesn't give me much cover, but I get out of the house and away from the guards without being seen, and head down the mountain. When I redial Declan, he asks me where I am, and if I'm hungry. And that's how I end up at In-N-Out Burger with Declan, Parker and Laurie. The trio is as weird as I remember. Possibly weirder.

They fight over fries and sauce packets for a full ten minutes before I clear my throat.

"Right, lass." Declan leans forward. The three stuffed into seats across from me. The better to steal each other's food, I guess. "Your pack."

"Shhh," Laurie cautions.

"Sorry," Declan says in an exaggerated whisper. "We got your file from the auction. Traced the address, but it was a fake."

I knew that. Xavier would cover my tracks better than that.

"So we asked the shifter slavers. Real nasty fellows, them. They didn't want to tell us anything, but we did some digging, and found your birth certificate. Selene Black of the Black Pine pack." He slaps down a document. I zero in on my parent's names.

I can't believe it. Lucius was right, these guys are good.

"From there it was easy," Parker continues. "The human news caught the massacre. A nearby pack had to come in and clean up—buy off the coroner and take possession of the bodies. Passed it off as a serial killer. Luckily there weren't too many fang marks to pass off as needle tracks or whatever. The leech who did in your pack was in a hurry, and sloppy. Did feed, left 'em where they lay."

"Y-you okay?" Laurie asks, putting out a hand close to mine without actually touching me.

"Yes," I find my voice. "I knew that. I have a picture of the clubhouse from...after."

"Right," Declan said after a long pause. "Well, we thought we'd spread out in a wider radius. Interview more packs in the nearby area, see if anyone knew what happened."

"Yeah. Sounds good." I cover my mouth with my hand.

"I'm s-s-sorry for your l-l-loss," Laurie stutters softly.

I jerk my head. "It was a long time ago. Do you think…" I swallow. "Do you think you could ask around to find out what happened to my family, too?" I tell them the date my family died. Laurie looks even more stricken. Declan glares at the table.

"Do you remember anything from that night?" Parker asks.

A flash of pain sears my temple. "No," I rub my head. "Nothing. It must have been traumatic. I usually get a headache when I try to remember."

Declan and Parker exchange looks.

"Do..." I rally before I lose my nerve. "do you think you can find out the vampire who did this?"

"I don't know, lass," Declan says grimly, a muscle clenched in his jaw. "But we're gonna try."

∾

Lucius

THE AIR of my crypt thickens as night falls. The magic that makes me what I am tingles along my body, waking my senses. I open my eyes. The night stretches before me, filled with delicious possibility. I have a pet to catch and punish, or reward.

I taste the air as I leave my crypt.

I fully expect Selene has run away. No worries. I will find her. I won't hurt her—I would never harm the little wolf, but I'm not finished with her yet.

I stop when I catch her fresh scent. Selene's room stands open, but she's still here, somewhere in the house. After all that's come between us, she didn't run.

"Pet," I call, stalking barefoot across the carpet towards the telltale sounds. She's on the Sybian, her hands and feet slipped through the bonds.

Oh fuck. Did it not release her? I hasten to her side. "Were you here all day?"

"No." She gives me a tired smile. "I left when the cuffs unlocked, but I wanted to be back before you woke. I wanted you to find me like this."

"Why, pet?" I stroke down her bare back. She's a miracle. I've never known anyone like her, not in two thousand years.

"I wanted to please you," she whispers, closing her eyes and pushing into my hand. She's in that sweet space after a scene, when her resistance has blown away.

"Oh, pet," I stroke back her sweaty hair. "You have. You do."

She whimpers as I lift her off the dildos. As I carry her into the bathroom she twines her arms around my shoulders, settling close until I coax her into a warm bath.

"I take it that you no longer wish to kill me."

"Jury's still out." The corners of her mouth tip up. "I talked to Declan and friends. They're looking for my pack. They told me they'd help me, and I believe them. I think I can trust them."

"You can. They help shifters of all sorts, and hate anyone who threatens the weak." My mouth twists is self-derision. "They owe me a debt, otherwise they'd never work for me."

"That's not true," she surprises me. "They spoke highly of you. Said you were okay...for a leech."

I chuckle and hold a bottle of water to her lips.

Her throat works, her eyes on my face as she drinks. When she's done, she lets her head fall back with a sigh. "So I guess we have a truce?"

"Truce," I agree. "Now hush and let me take care of you." She closes her eyes and I wash her, massaging her feet, her calves, her toes. She's limp and pliant when I'm done with her, her skin pink from the bath. I slide a hand down her inner thigh and she closes her legs, tucking away from me with a whimper.

"Poor pussy," I croon and give her a few painkillers. Her shifter healing has kicked in, healing her labia of all but some residual puffiness, but I don't want her feeling any pain. She lays back, lets me wash her hair.

When I lean close, her lips part, her throat working.

"Shhh," I tell her. "Just be quiet."

She shakes her head.

"Pet. Obey me."

"I watched the sunrise," she whispers, her throat hoarse. She sits up, capturing my hand. "It started with a glow. A yellow light on the mountains. The sky had already turned navy blue…"

I sit frozen as Selene describes the dawn, every minute.

When she's done, she licks her lips. "Did I do all right?"

I blink. "Pet. That was perfect."

∽

Selene

I WAKE to cool air blowing across my face. Beside me, a giant form breaks his stillness to stroke the hair back from my face.

"Pet. You're awake."

"You're still here."

"Where else would I be?" He keeps playing with my hair, spreading it over my shoulder, gathering it in his fist. He's obsessed with it. "You feeling all right?"

"Not dead yet."

We're together, alone. The room is familiar. The master bedroom, on the giant king bed across from the fireplace where I was trapped.

I guess he's forgiven me for tearing apart his bedroom.

I twine my legs with his.

"Pet, no. You're sore."

I take his hand and place it on my lower belly. "I'm ready. I want it."

Lucius slides his hand lower, eyes glittering. "You know, you're not really submissive."

"I told you that." I roll my eyes, my breath coming in pants.

"You've always been too brave for your own good. Even when you kneel for me, you show no fear."

I snort. "I've always been afraid of you. I'm not dumb."

He pinches my nipples. The pain rings through my body, sets my senses singing. I hook my bare leg around his hips, coaxing him closer, well aware that I can't make him do anything he doesn't want to do.

"I want this."

"So brazen." His lips nuzzle my jaw. I turn my head, chasing his kiss. He withholds it, dragging his lips over my face while he pins me with his heavy body, forcing me to accept his dominance. When he finally presses his mouth against mine, I let out a triumphant growl.

He finishes the kiss, gazing at me with satisfaction while his cock pokes my thigh, a hard, distracting length.

"You're an alpha, Selene. In any pack you would be at the top."

I flinch at the mention of a pack. He reads my dismay

because he slides his hand up my front. "Pet, I didn't mean—"

"It's okay," I interrupt. "I know what you meant. I'm not in a pack, now."

"No. You're here, with me."

"The home of the Vampire King."

"In bed with a monster."

I crane my neck to find his ear. I can't fight his pull, not any more. "There's no place I'd rather be."

With a growl of his own, he grabs my wrists, pinning them beside my hips as he works his way down.

"Be still," he orders when he reaches my pussy, his hot breath blowing over my shaved skin, making me try to wriggle out of reach.

His fangs scrape my bare labia, and I shiver at how dangerous he is.

"My pet, so sweet, so tempting." He nuzzles my inner thigh. "Do you know there's an artery, right here?" His tongue swirls over sensitive skin, followed by his nipping teeth. "Delicious. A veritable buffet, right here."

Do it. Bite me. I want to beg, but my pussy must look too juicy and appetizing because he turns his head and rewards me with a long lick. I've healed from the electric play the night before, but can't suppress a whimper as he lashes my labia with his tongue, driving me to the peak. His hands push apart my legs as mine fist in the sheets.

"Beg me before you come," he orders and I immediately start babbling.

"Please..sir, Lucius…"

"Come. Now." He accompanies his order with two

fingers pressing on my g-spot, and I come hard enough to crack in two.

I'm still gasping as he rises over me, grasps my wrists again and fills me. I've been stretched by his fingers and dildos, but nothing prepares me for the feel of his cock: Hard. Dominating. Perfect. My eyes water, it's so beautiful.

"Pet," he rasps, rocking gently, surging into me as my orgasm builds again.

"Thank you," I whisper.

"Fuck," he mutters, eyes roving over my face. "So sweet." His hips roll against mine, sending his cock deeper. "You gonna come for me?"

"Yes—"

"Yes?"

"Yes, please, sir, may I come?"

"Good girl." He speeds his thrusts and my legs start shaking. "Come, beautiful. Come for me."

I cry out, head flying back as his cock rams my cervix. It's too much, it's not enough, it's just the way I like it. My nipples are chiseled points, rubbing against his firm chest as he gathers me close. His fangs nip my ear, a little pinch I feel in my pussy. He bites harder, sharp enough to break skin. "Mmmm," he murmurs, licking my ear lobe. I come harder knowing he's licking my blood, tasting me.

Lucius

. . .

My she-wolf howls under me, her pussy clenching me like a vise. The drop of her blood blooms on my tongue as I finish inside her. I reach between us, grazing her clit until she jerks hard, her eyes fluttering through her final climax. I lick my lips and pull out, admiring the glazed pink of her poor battered pussy. Her taste is addictive. I've never known anything so sweet.

I lounge beside her, trailing my fingers over her face, between her breasts, I could lie here forever, watching her.

But as always, my pet must push it.

Her arms slip around my shoulders and her mouth nuzzles my ear. "Bite me," she whispers. "I want to feel it."

I draw my head back to study her face. "It might hurt, at first."

She meets my eyes, fearless as always. "I can take the pain."

"Yes, I know you can." I lift off of her, signalling for her to stay still as I settle between her legs. "I'll make it good for you," I promise, working down her body. I penetrate her with my fingers, working her slowly to a peak. She responds as she always does, fighting the rising pleasure, making me wring it out of her. As she gasps through her climax, I flip her over and drive inside her tight pussy. Her inner muscles are hot and grasping, pulsing with her orgasm, squeezing me like a fist. I spear her, gathering her in my arms and bowing her body back. One orgasm ends and another begins, tearing a cry from my beautiful pet's chest. I wrap an arm around her middle, bracing and holding her up as I take her from behind. My free hand sweeps the hair away from her neck.

"Be still," I tell her, pinning her with a strong thrust. I grasp her neck, forcing her head to the side. "This will hurt a bit." My head whips to the opposite side, my fangs pierce her sweet skin. A pinch as I penetrate her, the promised painful moment. Her pussy clenches. I take a strong pull, pleasure blooming in my brain as the sweet rush of blood hits my tongue. Selene moans, and my fangs pump a pleasure serum into her body.

She comes, screaming my name, as I pierce her over and over with my fangs and my cock.

When it's over, I clean her off with a wet cloth. I make her drink a glass of water and take another Advil. I don't want her to feel the merest hint of discomfort. Unless I'm torturing her.

The bed dips under my weight, and she rolls down the slope into me. I kiss her sweaty temple. "How are you feeling?"

She opens her eyes. "I'm not dead yet."

I stroke her neck. "Are you sure?" I turn her jaw this way and that, examining the bite marks I left on her neck.

"Werewolves mark each other when they mate," she murmurs.

"Do you wish these were mating marks?"

"No." Her body hardens.

"You sure? Werewolves mate for life."

She turns her face away, giving me her profile. "I'm not interested in a mate. Ever."

I cup her chin, drawing her back to me. "You're so young, pet. You don't know what you want."

"I don't want a mate. I don't want to risk…"

"Losing them?"

She's quiet.

"We all die," I remind her.

"Except you," she mutters darkly.

"Except me. But even I could choose to face the dawn."

That gets her attention. "Would you? One day?"

"If I ever loved someone beyond reason. Beyond my own good sense, and they were mortal, then yes. When they died, I would face the dawn."

A furrow appears between her brows and I press my fingers to it, working to smooth it away.

"So, you see, you and I are the same. We both refuse to give into love. Do you know why?"

"Because we are incapable of being with someone?"

"No," I tell her what she already knows. "Because we love too deeply and too much."

She snuggles into me. "That's why I like this."

"Why, pet, I'm flattered. You like me?"

"No, not you. This." She presses into me. "Snuggling. With a vampire king."

"I can't ever let you leave here. My reputation won't live it down."

"You're going to kill me, remember?" she yawns. "Or I'll kill you."

"You speak of life and death so lightly pet."

"I'm ready."

"You're young," I remind her. "You shouldn't throw your life away."

"Are you lecturing me?" her eyes widen.

"Yes. You're wasting yourself on a stupid cause."

"It's not a stupid cause."

"Assassinating me? Foolhardy and impossible."

"Well, you would say that," she grumbles. "You don't want to be assassinated."

"Not only that," I say, and I'm surprised to find it's the truth. " I don't think someone as young and lovely as you should waste her life obsessed with me."

She gives me a look. "Obsessed, huh?"

I squeeze the muscles in her hands and arms. "You've fought before. Did you imagine fighting me?"

"Yes," she answers, tense.

"Don't worry pet. I won't question you anymore."

"You don't want to know why?"

"I've lived a long time. I've committed any number of abominations." I turn her to her side so I can spoon her. "You have a very human view of justice. Does the lion regret killing the gazelle? This is the law of nature. Survival."

"And if a lion kills senselessly, needlessly, should it die?"

"If it is stronger than its prey, than no. It has a right to kill."

"Is that what you think? You have a right to kill? Where is your humanity?"

"It bled out with my life when the vampire virus took over."

She stills. "So you don't have a sense of morality."

"I do, pet. I have been very moral, especially when compared with my colleagues."

"Would Georgianna say you're moral?"

I hide a smile. Selene's obsession with my past love is more telling than she knows. My little pet has feelings for me. "She might. I treated her well. I know you have no reason to believe me—"

"I believe you," she contradicts me softly and looks me in the eyes. No other creature looks me in the eyes like Selene does. Her lack of fear isn't bravado. She wants to look at me, so she does. She might be the only creature who truly sees me. "You treat me well," she says. "So I can believe you showed kindness to her."

"Until she betrayed me. I killed her. She tried to kill me, and I... well, I'm the bigger predator."

"You loved her."

"Yes. And I believe she loved me."

"What?"

"A vampire in love, is that so impossible?" I tease.

A little shake of her head. "She loved you and she tried to kill you? Why?"

My heart sinks, remembering. "Because, Selene, her maker told her to."

"Her maker?"

"He was a vampire like me, old, powerful. He brought her to life. Loved her, I thought, like a daughter. But now I know he wanted more from her."

Selene wrinkles her nose. "Eww."

"Yes. It's a tricky relationship, the bond between sire and sired, and he took advantage. He ordered her to kill me, and I doubt she thought to say no." My sigh gusts through Selene's hair. "I've never told anyone this."

"Why are you telling me?"

"I don't know. Maybe because you look just like her. You remind me how I felt when I was with her. Young. In love."

"Love."

She's quiet so long I think she's fallen asleep.

"Lucius?" Selene asks in a small voice.

"Yes, pet?"

"What happens after? Where do we go from here?"

"What do you want to happen?"

"I would like...there are things I would have liked to do."

"Kill me?" I offer, dryly.

"There's that...but other things too. Those shifters in cages. I wanted to save them."

"What if they wanted to be there?'

"They don't. The auctions are an abomination. I'd like to put a stop to them."

I want the same thing, though she doesn't know that. "How about...you help me, and I help you?"

"How?"

"You remain here, as my submissive, until the end of the month." That will give me time to flush out my enemies. "In return I will stop the auctions."

"And set all the other shifters free?"

"Yes. No shifter will serve a vampire. Not unless they want to."

"They won't want to," she says.

"You sound so sure. A shifter in love with a vampire? Is that such an impossible thing?" I ask.

She raises her head and meets my gaze. The air charges between us. Little currents of electricity running between me and her.

"One month," she agrees, her voice husky. "Then it's over."

"One month." I nod and pull her back into my arms. "Now, hush. We have things to do." I reach to the bedside table and nab the remote.

She hides her face in my neck. "No more scening, I can't take…"

"Shh," I chuckle. "It's all right, pet. That part of the night is done."

I click a button and a panel over the fireplace pulls back, revealing a flat screen TV. Another button and the screen flickers on.

Monty Python and the Holy Grail starts playing. Selene goes still.

"Comfortable?" I whisper. She nods, eyes on the screen.

"Good. Relax," I order. A moment later she giggles at the 'Swedish' subtitles. She's still rigid in my lap, fighting my order.

At one point she makes to move and I restrain her.

"I have to pee," she pouts and I let her go on the promise that she come right back.

"Feeling all right?" I ask when she re-enters and stands at the foot of the bed.

"Just a flesh wound," she says in the Black Knight's voice.

I open my arms. "Come," I order her when she hesitates. "I want to hold you." Biting her lip, Selene crawls into my lap. A second later, my submissive she wolf sighs happily. The credits keep rolling and our laughter mingles.

It won't last forever. But nothing does.

Selene

I WAKE at noon the next day. The bed is empty and I am bereft.

I didn't expect him to be this way. I didn't expect for the kindness, hate, anger and love all tangled up. But whenever he's gone...I miss him.

He says he didn't kill my pack. Who do I believe? My mentor, who sacrificed everything to give me revenge, or Lucius?

Do I trust my head or my heart?

"I'm such an idiot." I rub sleep from my face. I have a crush on the Vampire King.

A shifter in love with a vampire...is that such an impossible thing?

He's a vampire, and not just any vampire—the King. I'm a wolf. We're worlds apart, far as the sun is from the moon.

It's no use. I'm in love with a monster. And I don't even care.

∽

AT NIGHTFALL, Lucius finds me pacing on the patio.

"Pet?"

I push back my wild fall of hair. I bathed after my babysitters left, but didn't primp. I couldn't bear to be inside, surrounded by his scent. "You call yourself a monster. Why?"

"I've done things, Selene," he says gently. "Things I

regret. Not what you're thinking—but I have killed before. Hurt people. But it was a long time ago." He spreads his hands. "The world was different then."

Call me stupid, but I believe him. "What made you go to the auction?"

"I heard they were auctioning shifters."

"You didn't know?" Xavier made it sound like the auctions were Lucius' idea.

"I knew there were vampires with a taste for shifter blood who'd take consorts. But shifters are not our natural victims. I didn't know shifter slavers were hunting down the weakest species and auctioning them to the highest bidder."

"You didn't?"

"No. I confess, I had my head in the sand. But now that I know, I'm putting a stop to it. And not because of our little agreement," he adds. "I had planned to do it long before that."

"You did?" I shake my head, dizzy. Lucius isn't the villain Xavier makes him out to be. Is he?

"It's not all altruism. There's evidence my sired have latched on to a new scheme to rise up against me." He shakes his head, looking as if he's found a toddler finger painting on the living room wall, not a set of grown vampires plotting a coup. "A few of them got the idea that they could turn shifters, form an army to overthrow my rule."

"Turn shifters? How?"

"The same way humans are turned vampire," he strokes his chin. "Blood exchanges, followed by an exchange of heart blood that kills the new host, allowing the vampire virus to take over."

"Is that possible? Have you done it?"

"Turned a shifter? No. I would never. Such a creature would be ... an abomination."

I flinch.

"Not fully shifter, not fully vampire. More powerful than either. If it could be done, of course. Few vampires are strong enough to create more of our kind. It takes a strong victim, and a strong sire. Perhaps that is why my sired turned to shifters. They had no luck with humans, and decided to try with a stronger species."

"And did it work? Is it possible?"

"I don't know. I don't think so—at least, I doubt any of my sired have discovered how to do it." He pauses. "There is a way to make shifters as powerful as vampires. but no one knows it."

I take a step forward. "How?"

"Our blood." He enters the patio, coming closer I try to puzzle out what he meant. He cocks his head, looking down at me. "Do you want me to show you?"

∿

Selene

"Yes." I say. I don't know what I'm consenting to, exactly. But I'm in too deep to stop.

"Come to me." Lucius orders. "Closer. That's it."

"What...what are you going to do?"

"I'm going to drink from you." He pushes my hair

back from my shoulders. "Then you're going to drink from me."

"What? No—" I suck in a breath as his fangs sink into my neck. A small pinch and bliss, my body shaking with the heady feeling.

"All right?" he murmurs.

"Just a flesh wound."

"Your turn, pet." He slashes a cut into his chest, presses my mouth to the wound. The first taste of blood is sweet, sizzling on my tongue.

"Do you feel it?" Lucius asks.

I gasp as adrenaline hits my veins. My limbs tingling with an excess of energy. My heart seems to pump faster, my senses sharpening.

I am super Selene, warrior woman.

"Race you." Lucius points to a saguaro cactus in the distance.

I push after him, my legs pumping—and I blur. The landscape rushes past until I stop, staggering. I reached the cactus before he did, and I'm not even tired. My body pulses with power.

I turn my palms up and study them, shaking. "How long does it last?"

"Depends on how much blood you drink. The effects wear off, in time. Until then, you're as powerful as a vampire. Maybe more powerful."

I stare at Lucius.

"Run with me." He holds out his hand.

I smile...and take off for the mountains. His laughter chases me and I run faster, with him hard on my heels. He might be letting me out pace him, but he's right. I am so much stronger than I ever was. With this blood, a super drug flowing through me, I could take down a Vampire King...

"This way," he shouts, blurring between two boulders. I follow, ducking around rocks as we climb the mountain trail, red dust rising in our wake. The trail ends halfway, so I make my own way, leaping from rock to rock, scaling the cliff leaps and bounds at a time until we reach the peak. The stars are brighter up here, the moon close enough to touch.

A whoosh of air and Lucius is at my back, wrapping his arms around me.

"I can see forever," I whisper and raise my hands to the endless blue, drinking in the silvery light until he turns me to face him, fists a hand in my hair, and claims my mouth. I arch into him with a cry, exhilaration snapping through me, making me tear at his clothes. We fall, him cushioning me before I hit the ground, rolling under and holding my hips aloft until I free his dick and drive down. The world spins and the starlight smiles above us, but even as I ride him, I know it's not forever.

This feeling can't last.

"Thank you," I murmur to him, much later, when we're tangled in his bed.

"You're welcome, pet. But what are you thanking me for?"

I palm his cheek, holding his incredible beauty in my hand. "You let me into your world. It's a beautiful thing."

"It is. But you're not a creature of the night. You're made of light." He catches a strand of my hair between his thumb and finger, rubs it between them.

"Moonlight," I correct. "Lucius. I want to stay with you."

He releases my hair, takes my leg and eases me under him. "No," he says as he glides inside me. My legs open wide to accept him. I couldn't resist him if I tried—and I have tried.

I twine my calves around his fine, flexing ass. I don't want to resist him any more.

"Lucius," I gasp as he speeds the rhythm of his thrusts.

"Selene." He sets his fangs at my throat, and pierces as my orgasm blows up.

When it's over, I huddle in the shelter of his strong arms.

"Let me stay," I murmur.

"I can't," he murmurs. "Even if I wanted, you don't belong here."

~

Selene

A PALE FACE greets me in the mirror. A month as a vampire's sex toy has left my cheeks pale and bloodless as a ghost's, not that I'm complaining. Any exhaustion is wiped away as soon as I drink Lucius' blood.

I apply red lipstick—the color of blood and vampire dreams—and check the fit of my collar. Lucius has me wear it almost constantly, now. Our nights have become one long scene. Our time together is frenzied, desperate, both of us aware of the countdown towards the end. Lucius has me so well trained, I'm wet and dripping as soon as I hear his voice. He says my name and I'm on edge. He snaps his fingers and I come. We spend every waking moment together, and we exchange blood almost every day.

In a few days, it'll be over.

Lucius strides past my door, looking delicious in his suit. He's promised me a night on the town, a night of pretending to be a couple. We'll end at Toxic, like usual. He's opened the top half of the club, so his sired can mingle with humans and sip from the victims in the dark corners. The dungeon is still reserved for him and me. In a few days, his sired will gather and I'll have my first public scene. Our last scene together.

A phone rings in the house. I exit my room in a rustle of fabric, still slipping my earrings in.

Lucius is in the foyer, on the phone. "Theophilus?" he answers and pauses. My ears prick. Lucius' has shared the names of his sired and Theophilus is one he respects. "Where are you?"

"At the club," says the vampire. I hear him as clearly as if he was in the room. Werewolf ears are great for eavesdropping.

Lucius turns and meets my eyes. He knows I'm listening and if he cared, he'd leave. He doesn't care. In the past few weeks, we've shared everything.

"You should come here, now," Theophilus says, his voice tense. "There's something you should see."

We hit the club at half past nine. The dance floor is already a crush, the bar four people deep.

Lucius stops beside coat check. Ever the gentleman, he

helps me out of my wrap, his face a stern mask as club employees rush around, eager to do his bidding.

He guides me to a private booth overlooking the dance floor. "I have to deal with something. I'll be right back."

"It's all right," I tell him, sliding deep into the booth. "It won't ruin our night." The way his jaw is clenched makes me think heads will roll. Literally.

"Keep everyone away from her," he tells the guard, and strides away, straight through the dance floor. He looks neither left nor right, but the crowds part for him as if by magic. As soon as he disappears, I sink back in the booth, toying with the glass of Merlot a waitress delivered, suppressing my growing sense of foreboding.

~

Lucius

"What is it?" I snap as soon as I enter my office. Most of my sired have jobs at the club, and even if they don't, I require them to report to me in person regularly. I have a list of vampires who avoid or delay these meetings. Theophilus isn't on it, but he better not disappoint me tonight. I have little time left with Selene, and I don't' want to waste it.

"It came in an unmarked package, delivered to the club's doorstep an hour before opening. We've got footage of the delivery, but the person was on foot in a ski mask. Male, Caucasian, probably human. We're still tracking him."

"So what was the package? A bomb?"

"No. This." He holds up a jump drive. "We've already done a virus scan and it's clean. Empty except for one video."

"Play it." I cross my arms and turn to the blank TV at the end of the room. To the side of my desk, a row of screens give me a view of the entire club via security feed. People gyrate on the dance floor, human and vampire alike. It's impossible to tell the vampires apart unless you are one yourself. By midnight, the vampires will have chosen their victims and herded them into a private booth to enjoy a drink in private.

"Sire," Theophilus calls my attention to the main screen. The mysterious video starts with a flash of familiar white blonde hair. Selene strides on screen, dressed in fatigues and a black sports bra. She's barefoot, unarmed, except for a wooden stake in her hand. Someone off camera must direct her, because she nods and turns, heading to a man chained down on the floor. She grabs a hank of his hair and draws his head back far enough I see his fangs. He's a vampire and she has a stake. In one movement, she plunges the weapon deep into his heart. She cuts off his head and holds it up for the camera. The shot ends, and another begins. Same set up. This time, the vampire is female.

"Your Majesty," someone calls. Theophilus waves them away and closes my office door, muffling the sounds of the club, people having a good time. The security feed shows a bright-eyed, happy horde of humans, laughing, talking, dancing on silent repeat. I want to destroy this office, burn the club to the ground, with everyone in it.

Torture Theophilus for being the messenger, for witnessing my humiliation.

Instead I remain still and silent, watching my lovely pet staking vampires. Again and again and again.

The video ends with a close up shot of Selene's perfect face. She's younger, cheeks flushed and hairline sweaty from exertion, but it's her. She looks straight into the camera, a defiant expression that's all too familiar.

A garbled voice breaks the silence. "Who are you?"

"My name's Selene."

"What is your mission?" The camera zooms in further.

"Find Lucius Frangelico."

"And then?"

She doesn't hesitate. "I'm going to kill him."

~

Selene

Ten minutes without Lucius, and I'm bored out of my mind. Watching vampires try to seduce unsuspecting humans isn't my idea of a good time.

"I'm going to the bathroom," I tell the guard.

"Frangelico says you stay here."

I roll my eyes. "It's either that, or I pee on the seat."

The guard touches his earpiece. "We'll clear it first," he says. Good call.

The bathroom they clear has a luxurious sitting room attached to the room with the stalls. There's a couch and huge mirrors. The sinks are set into fancy marble topped vanities with gold faucets. I primp and freshen up, feeling a little bad that there are women waiting in the hall to pee while I have the entire room to myself. Lucius is paranoid about security, seriously. It's not like anyone can get to me and even if they could—

"Hello, Selene," a deep voice makes my head snap around. A whimper escapes my throat as a giant shadow pushes open the door and enters.

Xavier.

"What are you doing here?" Any minute my guards should burst in.

He prowls to my side and sets down a glass filled with amber liquid on the fancy vanity.

"Drink," he orders. "You'll need it."

I've swallowed half the glass before I realize I've obeyed without question. Old habits die hard.

I finish off the drink and set it down.

"You can't be here," I whisper. I stare in the mirror at my own reflection. Xavier's doesn't show, but I feel his eyes on me all the same.

"Frightened for me?"

I start to turn and he grips my neck.

"Have you forgotten who you are? What he did to you?"

"I've...gotten to know him. He's not like that..." I feel stupid even as I say it.

"He's a monster."

I blink as Xavier uses the word Lucius so often uses to refer to himself.

"He killed your pack with no remorse."

"Is there proof?"

"You've seen the photos. What more proof do you need?"

That's not proof, I want to say. But vampires can't be caught on film, so if there is any proof, it's lost. "Why did he do it? He can lure any victim he likes. Why would he need to massacre an entire pack?

"Who knows why the killer kills? Boredom in his old age."

I bite my lip because Lucius has said the same sort of things. I almost tell him Lucius has a search team looking for my old pack but Xavier speaks first.

"There's more. I have eye witnesses. He took the youngest and the strongest to his lair. Lucius took them to his lair where he drank from their neck, forced them to drink from him, then tore out their hearts."

I shake my head.

"Yes," Xavier booms. "It's true."

"Why would he do that?"

"To turn shifters into vampires."

"He can't do that. He wouldn't."

"If he can do that, he'll be the most powerful vampire on earth." He sets the stake on the sink. "Unless you can stop him."

~

Lucius

THE VIDEO ENDS and I rewind it. This time I play it on silent. Whether she's facing the camera, staking or beheading, her expression never changes. She's so young. So determined.

It's one thing to hear her admit she came to kill me.

It's another to see it.

She worked at this. Trained. Everything we've shared and she hasn't told me who sent her. I could torture it out of her, but it will break the fragile trust we have.

"I thought you should know," Theophilus says, stupidly reminding me he's here, witnessing this private humiliation.

I whirl on him. "Did you deliver this?"

He backs up, palms up. "No…"

"Did you have anything to do with this?"

"No! I just happened to be here. That's the she wolf you bought at auction, right?'

"Yes." I grip the edge of my desk so hard something cracks. "This video. Did it come with anything else?"

"Just the jump drive."

"Show me the box."

Theophilus hastens to fetch it. "We had it checked out when we first thought it was a bomb."

No return label, just the club's address scrawled on a white notecard taped to the front. I rip the tape away with a sharp nail. Peel off the label and there it is, the note. On screen his voice was garbled, but when I read the slanted script Xavier's voice plays in my head.

Quite the warrior, isn't she?
She was mine all along.

Selene

I BARELY REGISTER when the guard resumes his place at my side. Xavier must have paid him off. Lucius' security isn't as tight as he thinks it is. I should tell him...after I decide whether or not to kill him.

A frantic giggle bubbles in my chest. I press my free hand to my mouth. My right is tucked half under the fancy skirt of my dress, hiding the stake Xavier gave me.

What the hell am I going to do?

A vampire appears at my booth. Slim and dressed in a black suit like a secret agent, he beckons to me.

"I'm taking you back to the mansion. The King's orders."

"Where is he?"

"He doesn't want to see you," the vampire says. "I'm Theophilus. Trust me, you don't want to cross him right now."

I exit the booth on shaky legs and follow my guide out of the club. He shuts me in the limo. The divider's up so I pull out the stake and stare at it all the way to Lucius' home.

Who do I trust? Who's telling the truth? Do I listen to my head or my heart?

∼

Selene

. . .

THE HOUSE IS QUIET, empty. I creep through the halls, not glancing into the rooms. There's a cold smell coming from the master bedroom. I follow the scent trail, my skin prickling.

I enter the room I tore apart searching, the one where I got trapped in the false tunnel under the fireplace. The fireplace is the same, but the king bed is gone folded up into the wall like a Murphy bed. In the spot where the bed used to be is a stone staircase leading down into darkness. The cold scent wafts up from the crypt.

This is Lucius' lair. He left it open for me. For 1 second, I'm dizzy. Does this mean Xavier found him?

Left hand out for balance, I descend. The walls and floor are solid stone, cold on my bare feet. My skin tingles as I cross the threshold, a buzzing feeling not unlike an electric current. The sensation rises to the point of pain; I hold my breath and fight through it, my steps slow like I'm wading through water. All at once, the spell lifts and I can breathe again. *Vampire's as old as Lucius have more than the usual defenses.*

The air changes. I scent, rather than see, a great room in front of me. A light comes on, triggered by my motion. It cuts the gloom enough for me to look left and right, half expecting a giant boulder to roll out of a booby trap, like something out of *Tomb Raider* or *Indiana Jones*. Nothing happens, but I hurry on, my feet slapping against the stone.

His large form stands on a raised platform. A long stone rectangle, about hip high and ten feet long, is the only piece of furniture.

His dark hair falls across his brow. "Pet. You're here."

"The door was open. This is your lair," I say stupidly. Surprise makes me Captain Obvious. "It's...big."

He looks around as if seeing it for the first time. "I've never had anyone here before. I suppose if I had planned ahead, I could've decorated."

"With what? Medieval furniture? Torture devices?" I try to joke.

"Yes, well. No one expects the Spanish inquisition."

I want to laugh, but he sounds so tired. He moves, putting the giant stone rectangle between us. Grateful for the barrier, I walk forward, stopping on the edge of the raised platform.

"Why did you let me in here?" My voice echoes in the empty space.

"Why did you come?"

I pull my right hand out from behind my back and show him the stake.

"Ah yes." He runs a thoughtful hand over the stone slab. It's the size and shape of a coffin. That's where he sleeps, in a sarcophagus. Another layer of protection. Even if I broke into his lair, I might not be able to open the coffin without help.

"I've been waiting for this moment," he tells me and pauses, eyebrows raised like he's waiting for me to deliver my part of the script.

"I was sent to kill you."

"I know."

I step onto the dais, and walk around the sarcophagus. I'm close enough to stake him, which means he's close enough to reach out and snap my neck.

"I didn't live this long by letting my guard down,"

Lucius continues. "As soon as I saw Xavier, I knew something was going on."

I jerk back. "You knew Xavier?"

"Yes. He was Georgianna's maker."

Georgianna the vampire he loved. The one I look like. "He ordered her to kill you. You killed her when she betrayed you."

"History repeats itself."

I step closer to Lucius. He doesn't move. "Why did you let me close? If you knew Xavier was involved, if he sent me, why did you keep me here?" And not just keep me close. Fuck me, hurt me in a way we both like. Show me a world I came to love.

He turns slightly towards me. "Some risks are worth it."

My head tilts back to keep my eyes on his as I move closer. "Are they?"

"I've lived a long time, Selene. I know when someone's worth it." He extends a finger, traces a strand of my hair that's fallen loose from my tight ponytail. His smile is so sad it hurts my heart. He does something I'd never expect. Not in a thousand years.

He turns his back.

The stake is somehow in my fingers.

I come forward. It's now or never. I could kill him. That's why he left his crypt open. He's letting me.

I toss the stake onto the floor by his feet. It lands with a clatter.

Lucius raises his head.

"I can't do it," I say, voice echoing a little in this stone tomb. "I won't. I wouldn't be here except....Xavier said you killed my family, my pack. But then I met you and… I don't know what to believe any more…" I wait but he stays silent. "I guess you didn't kill them."

"Do you want me to deny it again?"

"No," I say, decided. "You didn't kill them. You've killed before but not like that. Not a massacre."

"You think better of me than anyone else, pet."

"It's not like you. Maybe before, a thousand years ago. But not now."

"I'm glad you think me so civilized." Light glints off his fangs, but he's not smiling.

"I've killed before. Xavier trained me. He found vampires for me to kill, and I staked them to practice for you. He told me they deserved to die." I trusted Xavier, but what if those vampires were innocent victims like my pack? "So I'm a killer, too." I swallow, working saliva into my dry mouth. Lucius still hasn't moved. "What do we do now?"

His cheek curves. "It's up to you, pet. What do you want to do?"

"I think…it's time to say goodbye."

He breaks his stillness, twisting around. His face is composed, regal, but his eyes are sad. "A vampire and a shifter. Is it such an impossible thing?"

My eyes drop to the stake. "Yes. Xavier won't be happy about what I've done."

"I'll handle Xavier."

I swipe a hand over my brow, drop it to my throat. My skin feels clammy. "He chose me because I looked like Georgianna."

"Yes."

"He's been planning this awhile." I gnaw my lip. "When I leave here, I'll have to go on the run."

He shifts his weight. "What makes you think I'll let you go?" Red light gleams in his eyes.

"You told me you would. You said the ones you love always leave you."

"They always die."

"I'm not going to die. Not for awhile. I can run." I suck in a breath, feeling dizzy. There's not enough air in this crypt. "I can't stay here. Vampires and shifters don't belong together."

He gazes at me, face limned half in light, half in darkness.

Answer me, I want to shake him.

"You're right. A vampire in love with a shifter. It's an impossible thing."

"I ...I just wanted you to know.

"Go. With my blessing."

I jerk my chin up and take a step. Like a klutz, I misstep and stagger off the platform. In an instant, Lucius is at my side, a big, dark monolith of support. His scent washes over me.

"Selene—"

"No—" I pull away. I'm not as strong as I act. If he touches me, I'll crumble. "I'm fine." I'm not fine. My stomach roils. My vision blurs, the world narrowing to the light at the end of the tunnel. I've got to get out of here before I do something weak, like burst into tears or vomit.

My legs wobble as I head for the exit, but I make it.

"Selene," Lucius calls after me. "Where will you go?"

I don't turn around. "Return to my pack's territory. See what happened to them."

"Take the blood. You might need it."

"Lucius—"

"Take it," he orders harshly, before continuing in a more normal voice. "And a car. My last gift to you."

I wait but he doesn't say anything else.

I want to tell him everything he means to me. Instead, I rally my weak limbs, my stomach still roiling.

He doesn't turn around or watch me go.

Fifteen minutes later, the night air hits my face as I stagger out the door. I make it to the side of the Lamborghini before leaning over to vomit on the pavement.

Several security guards pop up to watch.

"You okay?" One of the guards asks.

I wave my hand. "Too much to drink tonight." That's not it. The only thing I drank was what Xavier gave me. I must have caught a bug.

He fetches me a pack of wipes and bottle of water, points out the plastic bag stored in the glove compartment. I lean on the door, heaving air into my aching lungs. Would suck to throw up in such a nice car. But I've got to get out of here.

The sickness lessens long enough for me to throw my stuff in the back.

I've got the blood. I don't know why, but it seemed too good to waste. It can help me fight. If Xavier comes after me, I might need it.

The further I drive, the weaker I feel. I must have eaten something weird. If breaking up is making me physically ill, I'm a sentimental fool. It's not like we were together that long. I didn't expect it to last, did I?

I drive faster, my vision blurring. The sun's coming up.

I turn off the main road and find a sheltered parking lot near a nature walk. Weakness radiates up my arms. I'm super dizzy. I open the door and dry heave a little, but my stomach is empty. I flop back and shut the door, locking the Lambo before reclining the seat. I'm not driving anymore today. My body feels like it's been beaten and encased in lead.

I dump my purse out, reach for the burner phone. I should call Declan and figure out what leads he has on my pack, but I'm too tired. I lie back and and pull the towel over my face. *Just a little sleep. Just a little…*

Lucius

COLD AIR WAFTS over my face. This time of night, I'd be preparing for bed, checking my security, closing my crypt.

Tonight I sit like a statue, my fist curled on my knee.

She left me.

I text Declan: *From now on, report directly to Selene.* I give him the burner number and let the phone clatter to the floor.

My crypt is still open, but I don't care. It's time to sleep. A month of heaven, and I am back to feeling like one of the damned.

My life stretches before me, dark as a night with no moon.

~

Selene

As soon as my head hits the headrest, the dream envelops me like it's been waiting for me. I'm back in the battered activity room of my pack's hangout. Old pool table in the corner. Ansel Adam's print peeling off the wall. There are voices coming from all around. Outside and in the kitchen. The whole pack's about to come here and eat, talk, play games, wile the night away.

Someone's calling my name. A woman's voice, soft and light. My mother. I haven't heard in over a decade. I step through the door—and end up in my bedroom. I haven't been here since the night my family died. The room tilts—I'm sitting in my bed, upright, rigid, waiting. Someone's outside. An intruder.

"Who's there?" my dad calls gruffly. My parent's door opens. He's going to confront the intruder.

No, I open my mouth to scream. *Don't go—he'll kill you!*

"Selene?" My mother opens the door to my bedroom to check on me. A thud and my father falls in the living room. My mother turns, the door swinging wide enough for me to watch the vampire blur to her side. He's on her before she can turn. Her voice cuts off and she falls, her head at a funny angle. Broken.

The vampire comes into my bedroom. I'm frozen in my bed, my mind screaming, my muscles refusing to respond as the vampire crosses the room to my bed. His huge body looms over mine. "Georgianna," he says, and reaches out to touch my hair. And I see his face clearly—

I scream and throw myself out of bed, but he's too fast. He's going to catch me—

The room fades and I'm back in the pack club house. Bodies all over the floor. An old woman in the corner, rocking. "It was him," she says. "It was the one-eyed vampire."

I come awake. My whole body chilled, like I've been plunged into ice water. All around me, shadow dance, lengthened. It's not dawn, but sunset. I've slept the day away.

I slept and I finally dreamed—

A clanging noise breaks the silence, makes me jump. My phone is going berserk.

I answer before I know what I'm doing.

"Hiya—is this tae wolf lass?"

It takes second for me to untangle the meaning of the accented words. "What? Yes. It's me. Selene."

"Thank fuck," Declan mutters. "Been calling ya all day!"

I glance at the car seat where the burner lay. "Yeah, I fell asleep. I was super tired." I must have been exhausted to pass out all day and not hear the ringer.

"You with Lucius?"

"No. I left him."

Declan pauses a beat. A car enters the parking lot and does a slow roll past the Lambo. I twist in my seat, following its trajectory. It's a black sedan with windows tinted enough I can't see the driver. Something about it makes me tense, but it doesn't stop or park, just glides past and exits. Must have been a wrong turn.

Declan's talking again, so I focus. "Frangelico wanted us to tell ya. We found a woman from your old pack."

"What?"

"She survived the massacre. Was picked up by another pack, lived out her days there. But she told the story of the attack to the leaders of her new pack. I can send ya the recording."

"That'd be good. Did you listen to it? What did she say? "

"We did, lass," he says in a gentle voice.

I swallow, my mouth is so dry. I still feel weak. "Tell me."

"It was a vampire attack. Just one, but he was strong."

"He?"

"She describes him."

My gut cramps so hard I double over. "Yes?" I gasp. *Please don't say it's Lucius. Please.*

"It's not Lucius," Declan says as if he can read my mind. I slump back in my seat, my head so light it could float away. *It wasn't him.*

My stomach clenches but the pains are weaker. My emotions are wreaking havoc on my body. Either that, or I ate something bad...over twenty four hours ago. I shouldn't be reacting so strongly.

My first instinct shouldn't be to clear Lucius' name, but there's no changing how I feel.

"At least, I don't think it was," Declan continues. "She

described a big, powerful vampire, but this one had only one eye."

The dizziness is back. "What?" I snap, my hand gripping the phone so hard the plastic cracks. "One eye? You're sure?"

"He wore an eye patch, but in the struggle a wolf ripped it away. There was nothing where his eye should be."

The image from my dream blows up in my mind's eye. The dark shape in my childhood bedroom, stalking me after killing my parent's. The one-eyed vampire. Xavier.

"You're sure?" I whisper. If this is true, it changes everything.

CHAPTER 9

Selene

FIVE MINUTES LATER, I've watched the recording Declan sent several times. The old lady is a smaller and frailer version of the she wolf I recognize. She was part of my old pack. My parents had her babysit my sister and me a few times.

On camera, she's unfocused and confused, her story meandering until she comes to the details of attack. She tells the tale with the growing horror of someone who can never forget the atrocity they lived through. Someone who still has nightmares of their pack's slaughter. Her description matches the image of the old picture. Bodies lying on the floor—she was one of the last to be wounded, and she fell and played dead until the attacker left. When she describes the attacker, her words are clear: a large, male vampire with scars on his face and one eye.

I replay the recording a few times, even though I don't need to. She said it over and over: the one-eyed vampire. He did it. He had one eye.

Scars and physical build are easy to recreate as part of a physical disguise, but there's no faking that one damning detail. How many one eyed vampires are there?

Declan sent me the details of the pack who made the recording, so I can follow up, but I believe this account. There's no reason for Lucius to lie, to create this long con. And this old lady isn't the only witness. Deep down, suppressed until they appear only in my darkest dreams, I have my own memories of the attacker.

All these years. All the nightmares, night after night. Sleeping with a stake to protect myself from the vampire in the room. Not Lucius.

Xavier.

It was Xavier who came to my family home and killed my parents, did away with my siblings. Xavier who took me away for foster care to raise me until he was ready to train me to kill. But first, Xavier mind wiped me so I wouldn't remember.

Except I knew. Deep down I knew. I never let down my guard.

Movement outside the car makes me jump. A bird flies into the shelter of mesquite branches. The sun has sunk behind the mountains, taking away all warmth. The last dying rays slant through the park, the world holding its breath before plunging into night.

I dial up Declan. I don't know why. I need to talk to someone.

He answers without a greeting. "Did ya watch it?"

"Yes." My voice must be thick with grief because his softens.

"I'm sorry, lass."

"It's okay. I'll be okay. I had a dream actually. Xavier killed my family and wiped my mind so I wouldn't remember. He returned and killed my pack. He took me and raised me…" I have to swallow several times to wet my throat enough to continue. "He told me Lucius did it. He promised me revenge, but all the while it was Xavier who killed them…" Because of Georgianna, I realize. He wanted to avenge her death, and when he found me, a girl who looked like her, he set his plan in motion. All those years for one long con.

Declan is silent, as if shocked by the turn of events. I can't blame him. I lived through it and I still find it horrifying.

"What ya goin tae do now?"

Good question. Easy answer. My mission hasn't changed, just my target.

I'm about to tell him to get intel on where Xavier is when an SUV screeches into the lot. In a cloud of dust, an escalade pulls up and parks behind me, blocking me in.

"Declan," I croak. "I've got company. I gotta call you back."

"What do ya mean, company?" His voice gets high and tiny as I toss the burner on the seat beside me. The escalade looms in the rearview mirror. Doors open and shadows stream out of it. My visitors aren't human.

My stomach starts roiling again. As if in a dream, I twist and grab the cooler on the car floor. *Take the blood. You might need it.*

Lucius knew this moment would come. My bad luck that it happened sooner rather than later.

Eyes on the vampires surrounding the car, I grab the first bag and uncap it.

A vampire knocks on my window. "Get out, sweetheart. Xavier wants to talk to you."

Bottoms up. I tip my head back and swallow the thick liquid as fast as I can. Maybe I'm too desperate to be grossed out, but the bittersweet taste isn't unpleasant. As soon as it pours down my throat, adrenaline floods my system. Time slows. The vampires blurring from the Escalade to my car seem to walk at a normal pace. My limbs, a second ago weak and shaky, feel stronger than ever.

My last gift to you.

I can fight anything off, even a vampire. Which is good, because in about two minutes I'm going to have to fight a lot of them.

"Come on," the vampire knocks again. His buddies are now armed with crowbars. Shame to use them on the Lambo, but I'm not getting out of the car. Not until I've downed more blood.

"Go to hell," I reply, and grab a second bag.

The world slows.

Moonlight glints on the leader's fangs. "Your funeral." He grabs his colleague's crowbar—the blurred movement almost at normal speed to my enhanced vision—and leaps on the car. A thud as the hood takes his body weight, and another as he brings the crowbar down onto the windshield. The glass cracks but doesn't shatter right away. Must be reinforced.

I wait as the vampire brings down the metal rod again and again. His buds stand back and watch the show. Not that they can pick the lock while their leader is destroying this beautiful car. Xavier must want me dead or alive—and I don't blame him. If I plotted and planned, killed and manipulated for a decade, only to have my quest for revenge thwarted by a single she wolf, I'd be mad too.

Not as mad as said she wolf. The blood of a Vampire King sizzles through my veins, augmenting my boiling rage. I'm going to get out of here, track and kill Xavier. First I have to deal with these thugs. It'll be a nice warm up.

Above me, the vampire grunts and brings down the crowbar hard enough to make the Lambo shudder. The glass is a fractured cobweb above my head. Any moment it'll shatter.

I have to bite the inside of my cheek not to laugh. This is going to be fun.

The vampire raises his weapon again.

"All right, all right," I shout, pretending to be scared. "I'm getting out." I raise my hands, showing empty palms. The vampire jerks his head towards my door. I unlock and open it, swinging out slowly. The vampires stand back to give me space.

Mistake.

The vampire on the car roof drops to my side. "Xavier wants—"

I never learn what my former mentor wants. A crowbar can't kill a vampire, but grabbing and jamming it into their guts is a good way to get their attention. Follow it up by twisting their head around hard enough to break their neck, and they drop neatly, ready to be staked or left out for the dawn. I do all this, and I do it fast enough that I blur. When I turn, I take a second to register the shock on the waiting faces. I'm fast as a vampire. Maybe faster.

As if in slow motion, the vampires start to jump on me—too slow. I jump first. The crowbar disembowels a second, a third. I've lost the element of surprise, but I've spent years practicing fighting and killing vampires. Between Lucius' blood, and Xavier's training, I am unstoppable.

I chase two into the park and stake them with palo verde branches. I return with more quickly fashioned stakes and take the rest of the guys out. I drag them into the park, hiding them in a ditch. Hopefully, no human will find them before dawn comes and turns them to ash.

When I stick my head into the Lambo, the burner phone is bleating. I grab it and the cooler of blood, and jog to the now empty Escalade. I took the keys off the leader.

Declan answers before the first ring.

"What happened?' he shouts.

"Five guys, vampires. They tried to take me to Xavier."

"Tried?"

"Yeah. Well, vampire blood has its benefits," I say before I can think.

But Declan knows all about vampire blood because he sucks in a breath, then mutters in a chastising tone, "Girl…"

My stomach flips as I start up the car. I'm feeling better. Not 100 percent, but good enough to take out anyone trying to stop me. Including a vampire or five.

"Where are you? "Declan asks.

A road sign flashes by and I read it to him. "It's about twenty miles from Lucius' home. Why?"

"Because when you hung up, we called Frangelico. Was gonna try to track your car, so we could get in and help you out."

"So?" I reverse the Escalade. Not as much torque as the Lambo, but pretty spry for such a heavy car.

"So, no one picked up at the house. Not Lucius. Not any of his security team."

My heart thuds to my feet. "I'm going there. Now."

"Selene—it's nae safe—Frangelico would want you to stay away—" Declan sputters.

"He could be in danger." Xavier wants Lucius bad enough to kill my entire family and pack and wait years until I was honed as his perfect weapon. He's not going to stop now.

"Who would dare attack the Vampire King?"

"Xavier," I answer, my heartbeat speeding up with the Escalade. "Not just Xavier. There's a coup. Lucius' sired want to overthrow him. What if they're working with Xavier?" The more I think about it, the more it makes sense. That auction wasn't Xavier's doing. Whatever's going on, all Lucius' enemies are in it together.

I hit the gas and the wheels squeal.

◠

Lucius

. . .

I know the minute the sun retreats before the dark. My lungs fill with air.

The lethargy rolls away. I rise, pushing aside the sarcophagus lid. My morning ritual requires an act of supernatural strength. It should make me feel all powerful. Immortal. Instead I am drained. Weak.

I close my coffin and stretch out on it, hands folded as if in prayer. But who would I pray to? In all my years, I am closest thing to a god anyone will ever meet. Immortal, all powerful.

A monster, forever damned.

Cool air wafts down the hall. I blink, but don't turn my head.

The house is empty without her. My life is empty without her.

But not my crypt. Someone else is here.

"Lucius," Xavier's voice echoes in the gloom.

I left the crypt open. Two thousand years and I never let my guard down. Not until her. And when she came in, she brought light into my world, the likes I thought I'd never see again.

The shadows coalesce as the one-eyed vampire takes a solid form.

It's time for this to end. I rise to greet my lifelong enemy. "Hello, old friend."

∽

Selene

. . .

My foot hits the floor as the SUV powers up the mountain to Lucius' palace.

"Hang on, lass," Declan's voice crackles on the burner phone. "We're almost there."

Gritting my teeth, I take a turn too fast. The Escalade almost tips on two wheels, straightening with a jarring bump. *I'm coming, Lucius.* I don't know if he's in trouble, but the fact that he's not answering his phone, that Xavier's minions found me doesn't bode well.

"It's gotta be Xavier and all of Lucius' sired." I tell Declan to let him know what we're walking into. As crazy as it sounds, I believe they're working together. "There's one thing I don't understand. Xavier was Lucius' enemy. Why would Lucius' sired align with him?" I wonder aloud.

"Selene, there's something else you should know," Declan says. "I didn't send you the full recording, just the specific part where the witness named the attacker."

I rip around another turn. "So?"

"Not all your pack died in the massacre. The alpha did some digging some of your pack were taken to a private compound. This facility contained a lab and there's evidence that the they didn't die right away." he stops as if what he's about to say is too horrible to blurt out.

"Torture?" I ask.

"Not quite. The vampires had a purpose for stealing the youngest and strongest of your pack. We think the vampires were trying to turn them."

"Shifters can't be turned," I say on autopilot, even as Lucius' words echo in my memory. *They got the idea that they could turn shifters,* he said. *Form an army to overthrow my rule.*

"Xavier was searching for a way. Had a theory that if a shifter could become a vampire, they'd be more powerful than any other creature on earth. Able to overthrow anyone."

"Like the Vampire King."

"Exactly."

"Did it work? Did any of the experiments work?"

"Apparently not. All the test subjects he stole eventually died. I'm sorry, lass."

"It's all right." *I thought they were dead long ago. This doesn't change anything.*

"Did he ever try to change you?"

"No." *I look like Lucius' first love. I was too precious to waste on a risky experiment. Unlike the rest of my pack.*

Fucking, fucking vampires. The SUV stinks of them. I hit the down buttons on the windows and relax as fresh air blows through the cabin.

I don't know if I can take on Xavier and all his sired, but I'm gonna try.

I slow as I approach the gate to Lucius' home. It's open, but someone's manning the guardhouse. "Quiet," I order Declan and roll the windows back up before I stop beside the guardhouse. A vampire exits.

"Did you get her? Xavier wants you to go on through—"

I slam open the door with enough force to drive him backwards. He stumbles and falls. With my enhanced vision, these vampires aren't so graceful. I fly out of the car and leap on top of him, snapping his neck before he can say a word. I stake him and leave him where he falls.

Behind the guardhouse, in a ditch, lie Lucius' guards. Not a good sign.

I hop back into the Escalade and tell this to Declan and he relays it to whoever's driving him.

"I'm going in," I say and toss the phone down.

"Wait for us, lass—" Declan cries and I shout back, "There's no time!"

A dark obstacle appears ahead. Two more black Escalades are parked to block the road. I almost slow—until I see the two shadows standing to the side. Vampire guards. One waves at me to stop. The other has a walkie talkie to his head. I see the moment they realize I'm not one of their colleagues. Their eyes widen.

"Oh no, you don't," I mutter, and mash the gas pedal down. My SUV hits the road block, metal on metal screeching in an earsplitting sound. The momentum blasts me past the two SUVs. I look back as the Escalade hurtles onward, but there's no sign of the vampires. It's too much to hope I got them in the crash.

A thump on the roof above my head, and I know exactly where one of the vampires went. I wrench the steering wheel back and forth, weaving up the steep incline, trying to shake the intruder off. The vampire sticks like a leech. I take a deep breath and jerk the wheel hard. The vehicle shudders, dancing out of control. The tires leave the road. My whole body is suspended in air for a horrible second as the SUV tips onto its right side, rolling several times before settling in a ditch.

Lucius

Xavier enters my crypt, his footsteps heavy. Like me, he can move soundlessly. It's a display of power when he chooses not to.

He regards my austere lair with a sneer and says, "I was never your friend."

I spread my hands. "Brother, then."

"You killed our sired."

"I've killed a lot of people. Most of them deserved it."

"A vampire with a conscience." Xavier shakes his head. "So superior."

"There's enough evil in the world without corrupting innocents. Although, I've corrupted my fair share."

The edges of his mouth curl. "I remember. There was a sweet little blonde you hunted, once."

"Georgianna. Yes. You turned her before I could."

"She was mine." Xavier's voice echoes through the crypt. He seems to realize he's lost his temper because he heaves a breath and straightens. "Just as Selene was mine."

"Was?" I tilt my head.

"I assume you killed her. Betrayal cannot go unpunished."

I incline my head, pretending to agree. "Forget the she wolf. She means nothing to me." The lie is ash in my mouth, but it's safer this way.

Xavier chuckles. "She played her part. You always were a soft touch. Why else would you have left your crypt open?"

"Maybe I'm ready for the end game." I set my hands

on my sarcophagus and lean forward. "So you decided to kill me. Tell me, Xavier, what makes you think you're strong enough to best me?"

"Interesting accusation coming from someone grieving for a lost pet. You can't even keep your sired in line."

"I like giving them a long leash."

"You coddle them. If they were mine—"

"Ahh but they are not. As I recall, you have trouble siring vampires. It requires too much...coddling."

"I sired Georgianna." Xavier's empty smile turns smug.

My hands clench to fists. "Only because I prepared her. You knew she'd consented to be turned. We'd completed blood exchanges. All that was left was the final exchange."

"It was so easy to seduce her away." His laugh fills the cavernous room.

"You mind wiped her."

"Of course I did," Xavier spreads his hands. "We are gods. To have that power and not use it?"

"It's not real. They do not consent."

"Consent," Xavier scoffs. "You want them to love you of their own free will."

"Yes."

"Another weakness. And how has it worked for you? How many sired have turned on you like you turned on our maker? How many have you killed?"

I don't answer.

Xavier ambles closer to the dais. "Georgianna didn't want to kill you, did you know that? I had to mind wipe her several times before she obeyed."

He's trying to make me angry. It's working.

"But she did obey, in the end. And you killed her. Amusing how history repeats itself?"

"I find it tiring." And I do. This whole miserable existence is not worth leaving the grave. It wasn't until Selene came into my world that I had a reason to feel. To walk a new path.

"You just need a challenge."

"Is that what I am to you, Xavier? A challenge?" I spread my hands. "How exactly did you think you could kill me?"

"Do you know how the shifter auctions came about?"

I narrow my eyes. "Some of my sired got a taste for shifter blood."

"Yes. Do you know how?"

I do, actually. My own research and interrogations have told me. But I fold my arms and let Xavier have his fun.

"I've been at it for years. Hunting shifters, capturing them. I thought, if I can get one to complete the change, I could create an army more powerful than anything on earth. There had to be a way to do it. We tried with all types of shifters, strong ones and weak ones. But they'd rather die as shifters than live again as the undead."

I snort, and he nods as if I've agreed.

"It is too bad. We could've created vampires faster than you could dream. An army of the strongest creatures on earth."

"So that was your plan to overthrow me?"

Xavier smiles. "Not the only one."

Selene

When I come to, I'm hanging upside down. I'm in a crushed cab, covered in glass. Windshield wiper fluid drains out of the hood. Where am I? What just happened? The road block. The car crash. The vampire—Vampire!

I rip away the seatbelt and gravity takes over. I fall, hit the roof of the destroyed Escalade. My world tilts. Blindly, I grope for the door lock. When I find the window opener, I say a prayer and press it. It opens most of the way.

I've contorted around to squeeze out of the window when hands clamp under my armpits. I save my strength and let the vampire drag me out. He tries to grab my throat but I'm too fast for him. I rear back and kick him in the gut. He falls. My speed is wearing off, but these guys aren't expecting me to be as fast as a vampire. I still have the element of surprise. I stake my fallen enemy and scramble away from the upside down SUV. There was another one.

I jog back to the scene of broken Escalades. Glass crunches under my shoes. I find the second vampire unconscious from the crash and finish him with one of my makeshift stakes.

The walkie talkie crackles on the ground with someone asking for updates. Any moment, they'll dispatch someone to check this out. Maybe they already have.

I've got to get out of here, but my sickness is back with a vengeance. My vision blurs.

Something white streaks up the road, solidifying into a

Camaro. I jolt backwards, falling into a ready fighting stance, but an Irish accent makes me pause.

"It's all right, lass! It's just us!"

The doors slam and gravel crunches as I stagger. Declan and Parker appear at my side.

"Easy, there, it's all right." They support me as I dry heave onto the dirt. I can't believe my stomach is still upset. It's been over twenty four hours that I've eaten anything.

"Thanks, " I say, using a section of my shirt to wipe my face.

"You all right?"

"No," I mumble. "I'm...I don't feel well."

"Come on, lass. Into the Camaro."

"Need to go to Lucius."

"You're in no condition to get to him."

Laurie appears, holding something. The cooler. It survived the crash.

"Feck, Declan mutters. "Not this again."

I push upright and jerk my arm out of Parker's grip to beckon to the tall shifter. "Give me the blood. Now."

Declan blocks my way. "Lass, no. It's too dangerous."

"Lucius gave it to me. He knows...He knows I need it to kill vampires. Xavier will hunt me to the ends of the earth when he finds out I betrayed him." My head throbs. Whatever illness I had earlier, it's not gone, but buried under the adrenaline rush the vampire blood gives me. When this is over, I'm going to have a hell of a migraine. "This has to end now. Tonight.

Lucius

"You've wanted to kill me for what, a hundred years? A thousand? Since we were sired? You were always jealous of me, Xavier. Of course you had several plans to kill me. None of them worked."

"Mmm," Xavier is back to looking smug. "I had high hopes for Selene."

"And she didn't kill me. She got close, but couldn't bring herself to do it."

"Are you so sure?"

"I'm here, aren't I? And she is not."

"Ah yes, there is that. Tell me, what exactly happened to her?" Xavier steps onto the dais, close enough for me to make out the scars on his face, even in the dim light. He lost his eye in a fight with a she-bear shifter, and even though he always wears a black eye patch, his face is a gruesome sight.

But his face doesn't hold my attention.

Behind him, in the hall, a shadow moves. A glimmer of a white blonde head. Xavier and I are no longer alone. My pet sneaked into the room.

She's come back to me at the best and worst possible moment.

Everything's changed.

∼

Selene

. . .

Xavier stands in front of the sarcophagus talking to Lucius like they're at a party. Vampires are nuts.

I snuck through the house. It was easy. I'd lived there almost a month, after all. Xavier's guards were alert and on edge, but they didn't expect me. No one expects a she-wolf hopped up on vampire blood. I left a trail of bodies.

"She's dead," Lucius' voice echoes around me. "I killed her."

"I thought you would. How'd she taste? I've always wondered." My ex-mentor's voice makes my skin crawl. "All those years keeping her untouched, unblooded. Chaste for the auction. How did you find her blood?"

Lucius licks his lips with an obscene flash of fang. "Delicious."

"Did you drain her?"

"Yes, I—" Lucius stops mid sentence as his whole body jerks. He slumps onto the sarcophagus, suddenly gasping for breath. I freeze.

"Ah yes. I was wondering when it would take effect." Xavier steps forward. He's inching towards Lucius.

"Stay back," rasps Lucius. I get to my feet. Something's happening. Should I go to him? I creep further into the room and Lucius puts up a hand. "Stay back," he repeats, even though Xavier hasn't moved. Lucius knows I'm here. The message was for me.

"Aren't you going to ask me what's going on?" Xavier chuckles. "Right now your limbs should be feeling heavy. The poison is delayed, but once it overwhelms your organs there's no going back. No antidote."

"Selene," Lucius whispers. My hairs stand on end. I rise. "No," Lucius orders, his voice sharp as a whip. I stay where I am, standing in plain sight, but Xavier's focused on his enemy.

"It's no use," Xavier says softly. "The poison's in your veins. I knew you wouldn't resist drinking from our Selene. Draining her dry. I had to be careful of the dose—enough to kill you without killing the shifter carrier too quickly. My lab worked for years to make it slow acting."

"When—" Lucius croaks.

My mind is racing ahead, knowing what Xavier will say. He poisoned me. That bastard poisoned me.

"At your club. I walked right in and gave her a drink. That's what one does at clubs, correct? Then you both went home and I just had to wait."

Lucius shudders. "Go on," he makes a chopping motion with his hand. He's ordering me to leave. I can't believe Xavier hasn't realized I'm here, but he's too focused on his enemy. "Make it quick—"

"Oh I don't think so," Xavier whispers "That's the beauty of it. With you weak, I can take my time." His body tenses and I know he's going to leap over the sarcophagus and take Lucius down.

"No!" With my remaining strength, I blur onto the platform to grab my ex mentor.

"Pet!" Lucius cries. "No!"

I'm faster than Xavier, but only just. I pull him back from attacking Lucius and he whirls, hissing. Too late, I see the stake in his hand.

Lucius

. . .

For an awful second, Selene and Xavier grapple, the huge vampire's body covering hers. I seize the stake she left at my feet a lifetime ago and leap over the stone coffin. I rip Xavier off Selene and slam the stake into his chest. He arches, stiffening, and falls. The stake isn't quite in his heart, but it'll hold him for now.

I whirl and crouch beside Selene.

"Hey." Her smile lights her entire face. Her small hand pats my bare chest. "He didn't get you."

"No."

From her shoulders up she's beautiful, her hair falling around her face, silken silver. It spills over her chest and when I brush it away, the locks come away stained with blood. Xavier buried a stake in her gut. I place a hand on her chest but don't dare tug the wood away. If he didn't hit an artery, he came close and removing the stake will speed the blood loss. Her limbs are cold, stiffening.

"What's happening?" Her lips turn blue.

"Pet…" My hands comb over her body, checking for more wounds. The stake shouldn't slow her shifter healing. She's fading too fast.

"The poison," Xavier cackles beside us.

I blur to his side. The stake is half in his heart. I set my foot on it and press. "Where's the antidote?"

His head rolls to the left and right. "There is none."

"Lucius…" Selene rasps.

Xavier grimaces. With his final strength, he lifts his hand and clutches my leg. "She's alive. How—?"

I lean over him, fangs bared. "I didn't kill her. I made

her mine." His grip convulses on my leg, but his strength is gone. Another enemy, vanquished. But at what cost?

"I'll see you in hell," I tell him and push the stake in another two inches, until his mouth slackens and his eyes go black.

I blur to Selene's side. "Baby. Sweet Selene. My pet." My hands stroke over her body. I want to carry her out, move her from this place, but she might not survive.

"Just a flesh wound..." she whispers. "Why are you...so sad..."

I shake my head, not wanting to answer. "Doesn't matter. You're here. How did—"

"Nobody expects the Spanish—" Blood leaks from her mouth and I stop her lips with two fingers.

"Shhhh. Don't talk." A tremor goes through her and I answer the question in her eyes. "You're body is shutting down. He poisoned you."

Her mouth works under my fingers. "Tried..."

"Yes, baby. He poisoned you to get to me." She's dying and it's my fault. It always is. My chest constricts, my body tightening with the need to roar.

Footsteps in the hall make me jerk upright. Declan and Parker and their tall, strange friend run up to the dais and take in the scene with horrified faces.

"Is it the blood?" The Irish wolf asks.

"She took the blood?" I snarl. "How much did she have?"

"All of it. She took all of it," Declan says. The tall shifter beside him twitches. "Is that what's wrong with her?"

I jerk my head sharply. "Poison. Meant for vampires."

My blood won't save her. Her shifter healing is working but her wounds are too great. Her system is overwhelmed. Nothing can save her now.

Unless...

"Is there an antidote?" Declan is asking. "What can we do—"

"Get out. Leave us." What I'm about to do can't be witnessed by anyone but me.

"Sire—"

"Your debt is paid," I snap at them, cradling Selene's head with gentle hands. "Go."

"No." Declan sounds so stubborn I tear my gaze away from Selene. No one says no to me. "We're not leaving her."

Of course they're devoted. She inspires that level of loyalty without trying.

"I would never hurt her. But you must leave. Leave and shut the crypt behind you. Tell no one what you saw today." The echo of my voice dies with the sound of retreating footsteps. I relax. Selene and I are alone. The only sound is the rattle of her breath in her broken chest.

"Oh, pet, you are undone." She's so pale, her life slipping away with every heartbeat. By the time her body fights the poison off, she'll die from the stake wound.

"Worth it..." she whispers. No anger, no rancor on her face. Nothing but love. She raises a hand and I capture it, bringing it to my lips.

"I hope you can forgive me for what I'm about to do."

Her eyes widen. "What—"

"Shhh." I stop her lips again, leaning close. "If you could choose, would you stay with me?"

Her brow quirks. "Stay?" Her body convulses in my hold as pain wracks her organs. The poison taking over.

"Listen, Selene." I'm running out of time. "What would you choose?"

Her mouth tips up under my fingers as she whispers, "You."

My head falls back, relief bursting in my chest. With Selene fading at my feet, I tear a wound in my flesh, right above my heart. I lift her and press her mouth to the red slash.

"Drink," I order. And her throat works, her lips sucking at my skin as she drinks deeply.

It might not work. It might be too late. But there's a slim chance and I have to try.

She convulses in my arms and I grip her tighter.

"That's it, pet. It'll be all right." She clutches me, straining. I tip her backwards so my blood flows more easily down her throat. The transformation takes several exchanges, sire to sired. We've exchanged blood several times, and with the amount she drank today, it might work.

But only if the poison doesn't overwhelm her body first.

A sigh shakes her body and her hands lose their grip on my shoulders. Her eyes close. This is it. Her organs are failing.

Hands shaking, I pull out the stake. Blood spurts, and I press my hand to her chest as she breathes her last. Her body can't survive the blood loss and the poison. But as she dies, the vampire virus will take root. I can only hope my blood will be enough to save her.

I can only wait.

In the stillness of my crypt, I hold her body for hours, long after she goes still. Long after the blood dries. Pressing a kiss to her cold lips, I rise and sponge her body clean. I lay her on the stone slab. In the grim darkness, her body glows with an inner light. A creature of moonlight, a beacon in the night. I could fall to my knees beside the sarcophagus and worship forever.

Instead, I clean the crypt and deal with Xavier's body. I wash and purify the crypt, and settle in for a long night. Over the years, I've held countless vigils, waiting for the vampires I've created to rise. The joy of their birth is always tinged with grief, their life predicated by their death. I bow my head in semblance of prayer. This crypt is now a womb.

Close to dawn, the silence breaks with a long mournful note. A wolf howling. The melancholy sound both a greeting and a goodbye. And I know.

Day is coming. I stretch out beside the sarcophagus and wait for the sleep of the dead. Above me, on the slab, Selene's body lies still, but I can sense the change. She's cheated death and come nightfall, she will rise as a vampire.

Immortal, like me.

∼

Selene

I OPEN my mouth and air rushes into my lungs. My body is

heavy as a slab of marble. I draw in deep breaths until tingles go up and down my limbs, bringing them to life.

I must have made a small sound, because the next moment Lucius stands over me, his forehead creased as he looks me up and down.

"Hey." I give Lucius a half grin. My mouth isn't working right. None of my limbs are. "What's happened?"

"Selene." There's a world of relief in his voice. "You're awake."

"Yeah. Captain Obvious." My muscles tense as I try to rise. Why can't I sit up?

"Easy, pet." He places a hand on my chest.

"I feel weird."

"Yes. I thought you might." He slides an arm under my shoulders and helps me sit up. My body feels different, and I'm not sure why. I'm naked, but surprisingly not cold. The crypt air flows around me, the cold vampire scent transformed into something warm and comforting. I touch the spot on my chest where Xavier stabbed me. The skin is smooth, unmarred. I am whole.

Lucius' hands skim down my sides. Blood roars in my veins, my body awakening to his touch. His chest is still smeared with blood but my own is clean. I swipe at the red stain and he captures my hand.

"What's wrong, pet?"

"So much blood," I mumble.

"Yes. It was necessary." He tilts his head close, his dark hair brushing my forehead. "You drank all the blood I gave you."

"I needed it."

He squeezes my hand. "You came back for me."

"You were in danger. In trouble. Xavier—" I push at Lucius, frantic to look past him.

"Shhh, he won't hurt you again."

My mentor is gone, the spot on the stones where he lay scrubbed clean.

"Is he..." I look from the stones to Lucius' shadowed face.

"Staked. I got him while he was distracted. I couldn't have done it without you, pet. You saved my life."

"Yes." Pain twists in my temple, I rub it away. I have to remember. "I'm glad he's gone. He killed my pack. My family. It was Xavier."

"Oh," Lucius sounds as pained as I feel. "Selene."

I shake my head and wince. "I'm glad he's gone." My head throbs like it's been clubbed. I sift through my memories, reliving what happened. Xavier, in the crypt, Lucius staggering— "He hurt you. You were hurt. You...when Xavier was here. You seemed to be weakened..." I stop as he smiles. "You were faking it! How did you know?"

"An educated guess. Xavier seemed so smug."

"He used me to try to kill you."

Lucius' smile fades. "Yes, pet, and I'm sorry. Your death is my fault."

I jerk in his arms. Bring my hands up between us, not to push him away, but to examine them. My hands look the same as they always have. A bit paler, perhaps. "I'm not...dead."

"Not in the way you think." He looks so sad, I cup his face.

"It's all right," I murmur.

"When you find out what I've done...I can only hope you can forgive me."

"Of course. What—"

In answer, he takes my fingers and puts them to my mouth. I don't understand until he pushes them past my lips. I touch something hard and slim and cold. Needle sharp. A fang. Not a wolf canine, but a tooth belonging to a greater predator, a—

"Vampire?" I ask, dreading his response.

Slowly, he nods.

A little sound escapes my throat. A whimper. A moan. "You turned me."

"I turned you," he confirms, and before I can say more, he gathers me into his arms. "I would do it again even knowing you'd change your mind. You said you wanted to be with me. I couldn't let you go. Not now. Now when I know—"

"Know what?" I turn in his arms so I'm facing him. My heart beats loud in my ears. Under my palm, Lucius' heart pumps blood in matching rhythm.

"I love you. Selene, I love you, and I couldn't let you go."

I raise my hand between us, right in front of my face. It looks the same, the pale skin, the bluish veins His blood flows through my veins. Immortal blood.

Everything is different. But when I retract my hand and see his face, I know: everything is the same.

"I know. Lucius, I know." I lay my palm on his cheek. His hair is tousled in contrast to his elegant features. For once he's not perfectly groomed. It only took a meeting with his enemy and a near death experience for him to forget his vanity.

He looks as beautiful as ever. Unworldly. A god come to earth. A legendary king come back to life. "I love you, too. I loved you from the first night."

His breath blows my hair about my shoulders. He embraces me, his lips finding my ear. "That's a relief."

I laugh into his hug. "Did you think I wouldn't forgive you for giving me life?"

He pulls away. "It comes with a price. Pet,"—he cups my chin, all seriousness—"I have condemned you to a life in darkness. You will never see the sun."

I lean forward and twine my arms around him, needing to feel him. "I do not need the sun," I tell him with all honesty. "You are all the light I need."

EPILOGUE

Club Toxic pulses with the music of the nightclub above. Below, the dungeon is crowded with vampires, all of Lucius' sired gathered at his command.

I apply lipstick carefully, blot once, apply again, until my lips are as red as the liquid of my drink. At least, I think they are. When I look in the mirror, I can't see a thing.

The hair raises on my neck a second before Lucius breathes in my ear.

"Nervous?" A firm hand squeezes my shoulder before sliding to loosely collar my neck.

"No." I keep looking at the mirror, even though I see nothing but the reflection of the room. I don't know why I even bother. Force of habit, I guess.

"Good girl." In the mirror, my glass rises in midair, lifted by an unseen hand. I take it, obediently.

"You look like a goddess." He dips close. "Maybe tonight I'll fuck a goddess in the ass."

I sputter and almost spill my drink.

"Careful." He steadies my hand. "You're too thin as it is."

"How much do I have to drink?"

"I will let you feed from the vein tonight," he promises and I shudder. That's the difference between him and other vampires, he explained. The new vampire is weak, dependent, requiring a balance of care and slow weaning into independence.

"Xavier tried to make vampires, but they either fought him and he killed them, or he mind wiped them and they didn't survive because they were too weak.

"That's why your sired survive?"

"Yes."

"So I'll survive?" I joked.

He didn't laugh. "You will do more than survive. You will thrive."

His fingers tip the glass and I let him help pour the blood down my throat. I'll do more than thrive. Already, my body is stronger, my reflexes faster than any vampires. I blur with ease. When we race on the mountain trails, I easily beat him, my shifter strength combining with the vampire abilities to create a new creature. I am unstoppable. The sired will soon outpace her sire. I am the most powerful predator on earth.

And totally in love.

"Ready?" He takes my glass from me.

"As I'll ever be."

He offers his arm.

"You don't want me to crawl?" I joke as I take it.

"Only if you choose. But not before them. Never before them. They will see you as an equal."

"They are not my equal."

His lips twitch. "No. But let them find that out the hard way."

"It will be my pleasure."

We step out of his office, into the light.

The crowds part as we glide past. There are plenty of curious glances. Plenty of hostile ones. I still smell like a shifter, a wolf. Another ability I have—controlling my scent. Only the most astute will sense that I am something more.

Lucius seats himself on the throne. I take my place at his side.

"Welcome, children. My dear sired." The crowd quiets as Lucius surveys them. He's not smiling, but I can tell he wants to. There's a touch of cruelty in the corner of his mouth. "You might be wondering why I called you all here. As you know, I attended an auction a month ago. I got a little carried away." A few vampires titter nervously, and Lucius gives an indulgent smile.

"This evening we celebrate a truly joyous occasion. I have a spectacle ready, the likes of which you've never seen."

I blank my face as the vampires eye me. They expect their King to show off his new submissive, and put me through my paces in front of them.

They're in for a hell of a surprise.

"Ladies and gentlemen, may I introduce Selene." Lucius holds out a hand and I place mine in his. "Your new queen."

Lucius

I SURVEY MY SIRED. Shocked, surly, they're murmuring to each other, reaffirming alliances. One wrong word and they'll rise against me.

"Sire," Theophilus steps forward. "Surely you don't mean to marry a shifter. As lovely as she is, she's hardly an equal—"

"I disagree."

Theophilus rocks back on his heels. He spreads his hands as if to say "I tried." The dissenting murmurs grow louder.

I raise my voice. "The shifter auctions are over. Anyone participating will be killed, except, of course, the shifter victims. They will be freed and paid a retribution sum. It will come out of the coffers of any vampire who purchased."

The room echoes with outright denial. Most vampires are beyond wealthy, but no matter the sum, paying a restitution payment to a shifter will hurt their pride.

Selene quivers at my side, ready to defend me. I place a hand on her back. I'll unleash my greatest weapon soon. "If you do not obey this command within the week, you won't just answer to me. You'll answer to Selene."

"You expect us to obey your shifter pet?" Someone calls from the crowd.

"Not just obey. I expect you to kneel."

The vampires recoil.

"I don't believe this," Dante pushes his way to the front. There's no sign of the fawning he usually shows.

"Xavier was right—you are weak." He whirls to face the crowd. "The time has come. The King has reached the end of his rule." He signals, and two vampires blur from the crowd, leaping towards me.

They never reach the foot of my throne. A flash of light makes the crowd scream. A second later, they're blinking and groping each other, rubbing streaming eyes.

The two attacking vampires lie on the ground, stakes jutting from their bodies. Dante's mouth falls open. The vampires who were at his back edge away.

"What's that, Dante?" I steeple my fingers. I cock my head and give everyone a lazy grin. They all can see I don't have a hair out of place.

A few seconds later, they notice the blood spatter on Selene's white gown.

"I know you planned to rise up against me. Xavier was a good choice for an alliance. Too bad he was ultimately defeated."

"You lie," Dante breathes. I fish an item out of my waistcoat pocket and toss his way. Xavier's eyepatch lands by his foot.

"Your plans have failed," I tell my sired. None of them are innocent of plotting against me. Even if they didn't participate in the plans for the coup, they'd didn't warn me, but waited to see which way the wind blew. Their silence damned them. "You will remain under my rule, and bow to me and my queen. Or you will die."

Dante snarls, "You're mad—"

I flick my fingers. Selene blurs from my side. In the blink of an eye she has the traitor on his knees, a stake a few inches in his chest and his head bent back at a painful angle.

"Shall I make an example out of him?" she asks, positioning a second stake at Dante's throat.

The vampires around her stir, stumble back. They didn't see her coming. Nobody expects a vampire-shifter hybrid.

"What is this?" Dante croaks. Even from his knees he emanates fury. "What have you done, Frangelico? Turned this she wolf into an abomination—" his rant ends in a gurgle as Selene stakes him fully. Blood sprays in an arc across the well dressed guests. The dead vampire slumps to the floor. Selene slinks back to my side, her white dress speckled with red.

"That was fun," she tells me with an impish grin. "Who's next?"

I raise my brows at the crowd. No one moves.

"I'm sure we'll root out more traitors in the coming months," I tell Selene. "Good sired are so hard to find these days. You can deal with them however you please."

"Thank you, Sire," Selene murmurs and runs her tongue over her fangs.

Theophilus is the first to sink to his knees. Slowly, the whole crowd genuflects to my beautiful queen.

I clap my hands. "That's done. Let's all have a drink." Club servants stream from the corners, passing out goblets of red wine. Two club workers start to remove the bodies and I order them away. "Leave them. An example. You can put them out with the trash this morning."

AFTER THE TOAST, the BDSM scenes begin. Vampires leave the dungeon and return with their chosen submissives. The club fills with the moans and screams of the damned.

Selene stands at my side, vigilant. She takes her role as my enforcer seriously. I bend my head toward her and she leans close.

"I'll need your help shutting down the shifter auctions," I murmur.

"My pleasure," Selene licks her fangs, watching a group of my sired scuttle past. Most bow their heads, but one shoots a glare her way.

"It may take a few more examples before they fear you," I observe.

"I'm looking forward to it," she purrs and I pull her onto my lap.

"Thank you," I whisper. Because of her, most of my sired will be spared. She will rule beside me, and all will tremble before her power.

"I'm with you, Lucius." she murmurs. "You will never again be alone."

"Light of my life." I motion and a club servant approaches, bowing. He holds out a cushion bearing a shining silver crown. I set the glittering diadem on her head.

"How do I look?" She turns her head so the diamonds catch the light.

"Like a queen." I grasp her chin. "A crown in public. A collar in private. You will kneel to me, and me alone."

She bites her lip. "I wouldn't have it any other way."

READ THE MIDNIGHT DOMS SPIN-OFF SERIES

We enjoyed the Club Toxic and the vampire world so much we decided to spin it off into its own series, **Midnight Doms.** There is one more **Bad Boy Alpha** book following this one (Alpha's Sun) and there's an entire new series, in which we've opened up Club Toxic to our favorite BDSM authors!

MIDNIGHT DOMS

Once upon a time, we vampires lived on the horror of humans. We lived for the pain, the fear. That BDSM has come so openly to the world has given us an outlet to continue to feed in the manner that suits us best—sweetening the feast with every stroke and cry, our victims becoming supple and willing, well-marinated meals just waiting for that next bite to be taken. We no longer leave large body counts in our wake, but we aren't half as civilized as we like to appear.

We are the Midnight doms. At night, we hunt. At midnight, we feast. Be careful, little human, or you might become our chosen prey...

(Excerpt above adapted from Her Vampire Master, Book One in the Midnight Doms)

-Join our Facebook party room: https://www.facebook.com/groups/701925946969115/

—Sign up to get news of the Midnight Doms releases: https://www.subscribepage.com/midnightdoms

READ ALL THE BAD BOY ALPHA
BOOKS

Bad Boy Alphas Series
Alpha's Temptation
Alpha's Danger
Alpha's Prize
Alpha's Challenge
Alpha's Obsession
Alpha's Desire
Alpha's War
Alpha's Mission
Alpha's Bane
Alpha's Secret
Alpha's Prey
Alpha's Blood
Alpha's Sun

ABOUT RENEE ROSE

USA TODAY BESTSELLING AUTHOR RENEE ROSE loves a dominant, dirty-talking alpha hero! She's sold over a half million copies of steamy romance with varying levels of kink. Her books have been featured in USA Today's *Happily Ever After* and *Popsugar*. Named Eroticon USA's Next Top Erotic Author in 2013, she has also won *Spunky and Sassy's* Favorite Sci-Fi and Anthology author, *The Romance Reviews* Best Historical Romance, and *Spanking Romance Reviews'* Best Sci-fi, Paranormal, Historical, Erotic, Ageplay and favorite couple and author. She's hit the *USA Today* list five times with various anthologies.

Please follow her on:
   Bookbub | Goodreads

Renee loves to connect with readers!
www.reneeroseromance.com
reneeroseauthor@gmail.com

OTHER TITLES BY RENEE ROSE

Vegas Underground Mafia Romance

King of Diamonds

Mafia Daddy

Jack of Spades

Ace of Hearts

Joker's Wild

His Queen of Clubs

Dead Man's Hand

More Mafia Romance

The Russian

The Don's Daughter

Mob Mistress

The Bossman

Contemporary

Black Light: Celebrity Roulette

Fire Daddy

Black Light: Roulette Redux

Her Royal Master

The Russian

Black Light: Valentine Roulette

Theirs to Protect

Scoring with Santa

Owned by the Marine

Theirs to Punish

Punishing Portia

The Professor's Girl

Safe in his Arms

Saved

The Elusive "O"

Paranormal

Bad Boy Alphas Series

Alpha's Temptation

Alpha's Danger

Alpha's Prize

Alpha's Challenge

Alpha's Obsession

Alpha's Desire

Alpha's War

Alpha's Mission

Alpha's Bane

Alpha's Secret

Alpha's Prey

Alpha's Blood

Alpha's Sun

Alpha Doms Series

The Alpha's Hunger

The Alpha's Promise

The Alpha's Punishment

Other Paranormals

His Captive Mortal

Deathless Love

Deathless Discipline

The Winter Storm: An Ever After Chronicle

Sci-Fi

Zandian Masters Series

His Human Slave

His Human Prisoner

Training His Human

His Human Rebel

His Human Vessel

His Mate and Master

Zandian Pet

Their Zandian Mate

His Human Possession

Zandian Brides (Reverse Harem)

Night of the Zandians

Bought by the Zandians

Mastered by the Zandians

Zandian Lights

Kept by the Zandian

The Hand of Vengeance

Her Alien Masters

Regency

The Darlington Incident

Humbled

The Reddington Scandal

The Westerfield Affair

Pleasing the Colonel

Western

His Little Lapis

The Devil of Whiskey Row

The Outlaw's Bride

Medieval

Mercenary

Medieval Discipline

Lords and Ladies

The Knight's Prisoner

Betrothed

Held for Ransom

The Knight's Seduction

The Conquered Brides (5 book box set)

Renaissance

Renaissance Discipline

Ageplay

Stepbrother's Rules

Her Hollywood Daddy

His Little Lapis

Black Light: Valentine's Roulette (Broken)

BDSM under the name Darling Adams

Medical Play

Yes, Doctor

Master/Slave

Punishing Portia

EXCERPT: KING OF DIAMONDS BY RENEE ROSE

Want to sample a new series? Check out Renee Rose's Vegas Underground mafia books including this book, King of Diamonds.

Sondra

I TUG down the hem of my one-piece, zippered housekeeping uniform dress. The Pepto Bismol pink number comes to my upper thighs and fits like a glove, hugging my curves, showing off my cleavage. Clearly, the owners of the Bellissimo Hotel and Casino want their maids to look as hot as their cocktail girls.

I went with it. I'm wearing a pair of platform-heeled wrap-arounds comfortable enough to clean rooms in, but sexy enough to show off the muscles in my legs, and I pulled my shoulder-length blonde hair into two fluffy pigtails.

When in Vegas, right?

My feminist friends from grad school would have a fit with this.

I push the not-so-little housekeeping cart down the hallway of the grand hotel portion of the casino. I spent all morning cleaning people's messes. And let me tell you, the messes in Vegas are big. Drug paraphernalia. Semen. Condoms. Blood. And this is an expensive, high-class place. I've only worked here two weeks and I've already seen all that and more.

I work fast. Some of the maids recommend taking your time so you don't get overloaded, but I still hope to impress someone at the Bellissimo into giving me a better job. Hence dressing like the casino version of the French maid fantasy.

Dolling myself up was probably prompted by what my cousin Corey dubs, *The Voice of Wrong*. I have the opposite of a sixth sense or voice of reason, especially when it comes to the male half of the population.

Why else would I be broke and on the rebound from the two-timing party boy I left in Reno? I'm a smart woman. I have a master's degree. I had a decent adjunct faculty position and a bright future.

But when I realized all my suspicions about Tanner cheating on me were true, I packed the Subaru I shared with him and left for Vegas to stay with Corey, who promised to get me a job dealing cards with her here.

But there aren't any dealer jobs available at the moment—only housekeeping. So now I'm at the bottom of the totem pole, broke, single, and without a set of wheels because my car got totaled in a hit and run the day I arrived.

Not that I plan to stay here long-term. I'm just testing the waters in Vegas. If I like it, I'll apply for adjunct college teaching jobs. I've even considered substitute teaching high school once I have the wheels to get around.

If I'm able to land a dealer job, though, I'll take it because the money would be three times what I'd make in the public school system. Which is a tragedy to be discussed on another day.

I head back into the main supply area which doubles as my boss' office and load up my cart in the housekeeping cave, stacking towels and soap boxes in neat rows.

"Oh for God's sake." Marissa, my supervisor, shoves her phone in the pocket of her housekeeping dress. A hot forty-two-year-old, she fills hers out in all the right places, making it look like a dress she chose to wear, rather than a uniform. "I have four people out sick today. Now I have to go do the bosses' suites myself," she groans.

I perk up. I know—that's *The Voice of Wrong*. I have a morbid fascination with everything mafioso. Like, I've watched every episode of *The Sopranos* and have memorized the script from *The Godfather*.

"You mean the Tacones' rooms? I'll do them." It's stupid, but I want a glimpse of them. What do real mafia men look like? Al Pacino? James Gandolfini? Or are they just ordinary guys? Maybe I've already passed them while pushing my cart around.

"I wish, but you can't. It's a special security clearance thing. And believe me—you don't want to. They are super paranoid and picky as hell. You can't look at the wrong thing without getting ripped a new one. They definitely wouldn't want to see anyone new up there. I'd probably lose my job over it, as a matter of fact."

I should be daunted, but this news only adds to the mystique I created in my mind around these men. "Well, I'm willing and available, if you want me to. I already finished my hallway. Or I could go with you and help? Make it go faster?"

I see my suggestion worming through her objections. Interest flits over her face, followed by more consternation.

I adopt a hopeful-helpful expression.

"Well, maybe that would be all right...I'd be supervising you, after all."

Yes! I'm dying of curiosity to see the mafia bosses up close. Foolish, I know, but I can't help it. I want to text Corey to tell her the news, but there isn't time. Corey knows all about my fascination, since I already pumped her for information.

Marissa loads a few other things on my cart and we head off together for the special bank of elevators—the only ones that go all the way to the top of the building and require a keycard to access.

"So, these guys are really touchy. Most times they're not in their rooms, and then all you have to worry about is staying away from their office desks," Marissa explains once we left the last public floor and it was just the two of us in the elevator. "Don't open any drawers—don't do anything that appears nosy. I'm serious—these guys are scary."

The doors swish open and I push the cart out,

following her around the bend to the first door. The sound of loud, male voices comes from the room.

Marissa winces. "*Always knock,*" she whispers before lifting her knuckles to rap on the door.

They clearly don't hear her, because the loud talking continues.

She knocks again and the talking stops.

"Yeah?" a deep masculine voice calls out.

"Housekeeping."

We wait as silence greets her call. After a moment the door swings open to reveal a middle-aged guy with slightly graying hair. "Yeah, we were just leaving." He pulls on what must be a thousand dollar suit jacket. A slight gut thickens his middle, but otherwise he's extremely good-looking. Behind him stand three other men, all dressed in equally nice suits, none wearing their jackets.

They ignore us as they push past, resuming their conversation in the hallway. "So I tell him…" The door closes behind them.

"Whew," Marissa breathes. "It's way easier if they're not here." She glances up at the corners of the rooms. "Of course there are cameras everywhere, so it's not like we aren't being watched." She points to a tiny red light shining from a little device mounted at the juncture of the wall and ceiling. I've already noticed them all over the casino. "But it's less nerve-wracking if we're not tiptoeing around them."

She jerks her head down the hall. "You take the bathroom and bedrooms, I'll do the kitchen, office and living area."

"Got it." I grab the supplies I need off the cart and head in the direction she indicated.

The bedroom's well-appointed in a nondescript way. I pull the sheets and bedspread up to make the bed. The sheets were probably 3,000 thread count, if there is such a thing. That may be an exaggeration but, really, they are amazing.

Just for kicks, I rub one against my cheek.

It's so smooth and soft. I can't imagine what it would be like to lie in that bed. I wonder which of the guys slept in here. I make the bed with hospital corners, the way Marissa trained me to, dust and vacuum, then move on to the second bedroom and then the bathroom. When I finish, I find Marissa vacuuming in the living room.

She switches it off and winds up the cord. "All done? Me too. Let's go to the next one."

I push out the cart and she taps on the door of the suite down the hall. No answer.

She keys us in. "It is way faster having you help," she says gratefully.

I flash her a smile. "I think it's more fun to work as a team, too."

She smiles back. "Yeah, somehow I don't think they would go for it as a regular thing, but it's nice for a change."

"Same routine?"

"Unless you want to switch? This one only has one bedroom."

"Nah," I say, "I like bed/bath." Of course that's because of my all-consuming curiosity. There are more personal effects in a bedroom and a bathroom, not that I saw anything of interest in the last place. I didn't go poking around, of course. The cameras in every corner have me nervous.

This place is the same as the last, as if they'd paid a decorator to furnish them and they were all identical. High luxury, but not much personality. Well, from what I understand, the Tacone family—at least the ones who run the Bellissimo—are all single men. What can I expect?

I make the bed and move on to dusting.

From the living room, I hear Marissa's voice.

"What?" I call out, but then I realize she's talking on the phone.

She comes in a moment later, breathless. "I have to go." Her face has gone pale. "My kid's been taken to the ER for a concussion."

"Oh shit. Go—I've got this. Do you want to give me the keycard for the last suite?" There are three suites on this top floor.

She looks around distractedly. "No, I'd better not. Could you just finish this place up and head back downstairs? I'll call Samuel to let him know what happened." Samuel's our boss, the head of housekeeping. "Don't forget to stay away from the desk in the office."

"Sure thing. Get out of here." I make a shooing motion. "Go be with your kid."

"Okay." She digs her purse out from the cart and slings it over her shoulder. "I'll see you tomorrow."

"I hope he's all right," I say to her back as she leaves.

She flings a weak smile over her shoulder. "Thanks. Bye."

I grab the vacuum and head back into the bedroom. When I finish, I hear male voices in the living room.

"Hope you can get some sleep, Nico. How long's it been?" one of the voices asked.

"Forty-eight hours. Fucking insomnia."

"G'luck, see you later." A door clicks shut.

My heart immediately beats a little faster with excitement or nerves. Yes—I'm a fool. Later, I would realize my mistake in not marching right out and introducing myself, but Marissa has me nervous about the Tacones and I freeze up. The cart stands out in the living room, though. I decide to go into the bathroom and clean everything I can without getting fresh supplies. Finally, I give up, square my shoulders and head out.

I arrive in the living room and pull out three folded towels, four hand towels and four washcloths. Out of my peripheral vision, I watch the broad shoulders and back of another finely dressed man.

He glances over then does a double-take. His dark eyes rake over me, lingering on my legs and traveling up to my breasts, then face. *"Who the fuck are you?"*

I should've expected that response, but it startles me anyway. He sounds scary. Seriously scary, and he walks toward me like he means business. He's beautiful, with dark wavy hair, a stubbled square jaw and thick-lashed eyes that bore a hole right through me.

"Huh? Who. The fuck. Are you?"

I panic. Instead of answering him, I turn and walk swiftly to the bathroom, as if putting fresh towels in his bathroom will fix everything.

He stalks after me and follows me in. "What are you doing in here?" He knocks the towels out of my hands.

Stunned, I stare down at them scattered on the floor. "I'm...housekeeping," I offer lamely. Damn my idiotic fascination with the mafia. This is not the freaking *Sopranos*. This is a real-life, dangerous man wearing a gun in a holster under his armpit. I know, because I see it when he reaches for me.

He grips my upper arms. "Bullshit. No one who looks like"—his eyes travel up and down the length of my body again—"*you*—works in housekeeping."

I blink, not sure what that means. I'm pretty, I know that, but there's nothing special about me. I'm your girl-next-door blue-eyed blonde type, on the short and curvy side. Not like my cousin Corey, who is tall, slender, red-haired and drop-dead gorgeous, with the confidence to match.

There's something lewd in the way he looks at me that makes it sound like I'm standing there in nipple tassels and a G-string instead of my short, fitted maid's dress. I play dumb. "I'm new. I've only been here a couple weeks."

He sports dark circles under his eyes, and I remember what he told the other man. He suffers from insomnia. Hasn't slept in forty-eight hours.

"Are you bugging the place?" he demands.

"Wha—" I can't even answer. I just stare like an idiot.

He starts frisking me for a weapon. "Is this a con? What do they think—I'm going to fuck you? Who sent you?"

I attempt to answer, but his warm hands sliding all over

me make me forget what I was going to say. *Why is he talking about fucking me?*

He stands up and gives me a tiny shake. "Who. Sent. You?" His dark eyes mesmerize. He smells of the casino—of whiskey and cash, and beneath it, his own simmering essence.

"No one...I mean, Marissa!" I exclaim her name like a secret password, but it only seems to irritate him further.

He reaches out and runs his fingers swiftly along the collar of my housekeeping dress, as if checking for some hidden wiretap. I'm pretty sure the guy's half out of his mind, maybe delirious with sleep deprivation. Maybe just nuts. I freeze, not wanting to set him off.

To my shock, he yanks down the zipper on the front of my dress, all the way to my waist.

If I were my cousin Corey, daughter of a mean FBI agent, I'd knee him in the balls, gun or not. But I was raised not to make waves. To be a nice girl and do what authority tells me to do.

So, like a freaking idiot, I just stand there. A tiny mewl leaves my lips, but I don't dare move, don't protest. He yanks the form-fitting dress to my waist and jerks it down over my hips.

I wrest my arms free from the fabric to wrap them around myself.

Nico Tacone shoves me aside to get the dress out from under my feet. He picks it up and runs his hands all over it, still searching for the mythical wiretap while I shiver in my bra and panties.

I fold my arms across my breasts. "Look, I'm not

wearing a wire or bugging the place," I breathe. "I was helping Marissa and then she got a call—"

"Save it," he barks. "You're too fucking perfect. What's the con? What the fuck are you doing in here?"

I'm confounded. Should I keep arguing the truth when it only pisses him off? I swallow. None of the words in my head seem like the right ones to say.

He reaches for my bra.

I bat at his hands, heart pumping like I just did two back-to-back spin classes. He ignores my feeble resistance. The bra is a front hook and he obviously excels at removing women's lingerie because it's off faster than the dress. My breasts spring out with a bounce, and he glares at them, as if I bared them just to tempt him. He examines the bra, then tosses it on the floor and stares at me. His eyes dip once more to my breasts and his expression grows even more furious. "Real tits," he mutters as if that's a punishable offense.

I try to step back but I bump into the toilet. "I'm not hiding anything. I'm just a maid. I got hired two weeks ago. You can call Samuel."

He steps closer. Tragically, the hardened menace on his handsome face only increases his attractiveness to me. I really am wired wrong. My body thrills at the nearness of him, pussy dampening. Or maybe it's the fact that he just stripped me practically naked while he stands there fully clothed. I think this is a fetish to some people. Apparently, I'm one of them. If I wasn't so scared, it would be uber hot.

He palms my backside, warm fingers sliding over the satiny fabric of my panties, but he's not groping me, he's still working efficiently, checking for bugs. He slides a thumb under the gusset, running the fabric through his fingers. My belly flutters.

Oh God. The back of his thumb brushes my dewy slit. I cringe in embarrassment. His head jerks up and he stares at me in surprise, nostrils flaring.

Then his brows slammed down as if it pisses him off I'm turned on, as if it's a trick.

That's when things really go to shit.

ABOUT LEE SAVINO

Lee Savino is a USA today bestselling author, mom and chocoholic.

Warning: Do not read her Berserker series, or you will be addicted to the huge, dominant warriors who will stop at nothing to claim their mates.

I repeat: Do. Not. Read. The Berserker Saga. Particularly not the thrilling excerpt below.

Download a free book from www.leesavino.com (don't read that either. Too much hot, sexy lovin').

EXCERPT: SOLD TO THE BERSERKERS

A MÉNAGE SHIFTER ROMANCE

By Lee Savino

The day my stepfather sold me to the Berserkers, I woke at dawn with him leering over me. "Get up." He made to kick me and I scrambled out of my sleep stupor to my feet.

"I need your help with a delivery."

I nodded and glanced at my sleeping mother and siblings. I didn't trust my stepfather around my three younger sisters, but if I was gone with him all day, they'd be safe. I'd taken to carrying a dirk myself. I did not dare kill him; we needed him for food and shelter, but if he attacked me again, I would fight.

My mother's second husband hated me, ever since the last time he'd tried to take me and I had fought back. My mother was gone to market, and when he tried to grab me, something in me snapped. I would not let him touch me again. I fought, kicking and scratching, and finally grabbing an iron pot and scalding him with heated water.

He bellowed and looked as if he wanted to hurt me, but

kept his distance. When my mother returned he pretended like nothing was wrong, but his eyes followed me with hatred and cunning.

Out loud he called me ugly and mocking the scar that marred my neck since a wild dog attacked me when I was young. I ignored this and kept my distance. I'd heard the taunts about my hideous face since the wounds had healed into scars, a mass of silver tissue at my neck.

That morning, I wrapped a scarf over my hair and scarred neck and followed my stepfather, carrying his wares down the old road. At first I thought we were headed to the great market, but when we reached the fork in the road and he went an unfamiliar way, I hesitated. Something wasn't right.

"This way, cur." He'd taken to calling me "dog". He'd taunted me, saying the only sounds I could make were grunts like a beast, so I might as well be one. He was right. The attack had taken my voice by damaging my throat.

If I followed him into the forest and he tried to kill me, I wouldn't even be able to cry out.

"There's a rich man who asked for his wares delivered to his door." He marched on without a backward glance and I followed.

I had lived all my life in the kingdom of Alba, but when my father died and my mother remarried, we moved to my stepfather's village in the highlands, at the foot of the great, forbidding mountains. There were stories of evil that lived in the dark crevices of the heights, but I'd never believed them.

I knew enough monsters living in plain sight.

The longer we walked, the lower the sun sank in the

sky, the more I knew my stepfather was trying to trick me, that there was no rich man waiting for these wares.

When the path curved, and my stepfather stepped out from behind a boulder to surprise me, I was half ready, but before I could reach for my dirk he struck me so hard I fell.

I woke tied to a tree.

The light was lower, heralding dusk. I struggled silently, frantic gasps escaping from my scarred throat. My stepfather stepped into view and I felt a second of relief at a familiar face, before remembering the evil this man had wrought on my body. Whatever he was planning, it would bode ill for me, and my younger sisters. If I didn't survive, they would eventually share the same fate as mine.

"You're awake," he said. "Just in time for the sale."

I strained but my bonds held fast. As my stepfather approached, I realized that the scarf that I wrapped around my neck to hide my scars had fallen, exposing them. Out of habit, I twitched my head to the side, tucking my bad side towards my shoulder.

My stepfather smirked.

"So ugly," he sneered. "I could never find a husband for you, but I found someone to take you. A group of warriors passing through who saw you, and want to slake their lust on your body. Who knows, if you please them, they may let you live. But I doubt you'll survive these men. They're foreigners, mercenaries, come to fight for the king. Berserkers. If you're lucky your death will be swift when they tear you apart."

I'd heard the tales of berserker warriors, fearsome warriors of old. Ageless, timeless, they'd sailed over the seas to the land, plundering, killing, taking slaves, they fought for our kings, and their own. Nothing could stand in their path when they went into a killing rage.

I fought to keep my fear off my face. Berserker's were a myth, so my stepfather had probably sold me to a band of passing soldiers who would take their pleasure from my flesh before leaving me for dead, or selling me on.

"I could've sold you long ago, if I stripped you bare and put a bag over you head to hide those scars."

His hands pawed at me, and I shied away from his disgusting breath. He slapped me, then tore at my braid, letting my hair spill over my face and shoulders.

Bound as I was, I still could glare at him. I could do nothing to stop the sale, but I hoped my fierce expression told him I'd fight to the death if he tried to force himself on me.

His hand started to wander down towards my breast when a shadow moved on the edge of the clearing. It caught my eye and I startled. My stepfather stepped back as the warriors poured from the trees.

My first thought was that they were not men, but beasts. They prowled forward, dark shapes almost one with the shadows. A few wore animal pelts and held back, lurking on the edge of the woods. Two came forward, wearing the garb of warriors, bristling with weapons. One had dark hair, and the other long, dirty blond with a beard to match.

Their eyes glowed with a terrifying light.

As they approached, the smell of raw meat and blood wafted over us, and my stomach twisted. I was glad my stepfather hadn't fed me all day, or I would've emptied my guts on the ground.

My stepfather's face and tone took on the wheedling expression I'd seen when he was selling in the market.

"Good evening, sirs," he cringed before the largest, the blond with hair streaming down his chest.

They were perfectly silent, but the blond approached, fixing me with strange golden eyes.

Their faces were fair enough, but their hulking forms and the quick, light way they moved made me catch my breath. I had never seen such massive men. Beside them, my stepfather looked like an ugly dwarf.

"This is the one you wanted," my stepfather continued. "She's healthy and strong. She will be a good slave for you."

My body would've shaken with terror, if I were not bound so tightly.

A dark haired warrior stepped up beside the blond and the two exchanged a look.

"You asked for the one with scars." My stepfather took my hair and jerked my head back, exposing the horrible, silvery mass. I shut my eyes, tears squeezing out at the sudden pain and humiliation.

The next thing I knew, my stepfather's grip loosened. A grunt, and I opened my eyes to see the dark haired warrior standing at my side. My stepfather sprawled on the ground as if he'd been pushed.

The blond leader prodded a boot into my stepfather's side.

"Get up," the blond said, in a voice that was more a

growl than a human sound. It curdled my blood. My stepfather scrambled to his feet.

The black haired man cut away the last of my bonds, and I sagged forward. I would've fallen but he caught me easily and set me on my feet, keeping his arms around me. I was not the smallest woman, but he was a giant. Muscles bulged in his arms and chest, but he held me carefully. I stared at him, taking in his raven dark hair and strange gold eyes.

He tucked me closer to his muscled body.

Meanwhile, my stepfather whined. "I just wanted to show you the scars—"

Again that frightening growl from the blond. "You don't touch what is ours."

"I don't want to touch her." My stepfather spat.

Despite myself, I cowered against the man who held me. A stranger I had never met, he was still a safer haven than my stepfather.

"I only wish to make sure you are satisfied, milords. Do you want to sample her?" my stepfather asked in an evil tone. He wanted to see me torn apart.

A growl rumbled under my ear and I lifted my head. Who were these men, these great warriors who had bought and paid for me? The arms around my body were strong and solid, inescapable, but the gold eyes looking down at me were kind. The warrior ran his thumb across the pad of my lips, and his fingers were gentle for such a large, violent looking warrior. Under the scent of blood, he smelled of snow and sharp cold, a clean scent.

He pressed his face against my head, breathing in a deep breath.

The blond was looking at us.

"It's her," the black haired man growled, his voice so guttural. "This is the one."

One of his hands came to cover the side of my face and throat, holding my face to his chest in a protective gesture.

I closed my eyes, relaxing in the solid warmth of the warrior's body.

A clink of gold, and the deed was done. I'd been sold.

When Brenna's father sells her to a band of passing warriors, her only thought is to survive. She doesn't expect to be claimed by the two fearsome warriors who lead the Berserker clan. Kept in captivity, she is coddled and cared for, treated more like a savior than a slave. Can captivity lead to love? And when she discovers the truth behind the myth of the fearsome warriors, can she accept her place as the Berserkers' true mate?

Author's Note: *Sold to the Berserkers is a standalone, short, MFM ménage romance starring two huge, dominant warriors who make it all about the woman. Read the whole best-selling Berserker saga to see what readers are raving about...*

The Berserker Saga
Sold to the Berserkers
Mated to the Berserkers
Bred by the Berserkers (free novella available on leesavino.com)

Taken by the Berserkers
Given to the Berserkers
Claimed by the Berserkers
Rescued by the Berserkers - free on all sites, including Wattpad
Captured by the Berserkers
Kidnapped by the Berserkers
Bonded to the Berserkers
Berserker Babies
Owned by the Berserkers
Night of the Berserkers

ALSO BY LEE SAVINO

Exiled To the Prison Planet

Draekon Mate

Draekon Fire

Draekon Heart

Draekon Abduction

Draekon Destiny

Draekon Fever

Draekon Rogue

Printed in Great Britain
by Amazon